Lines Within the Circle

A NOVEL BY

JEAN BONNIN

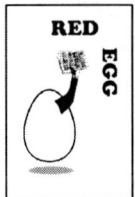

By the same author

A Certain Experience of the Impossible (2009)

Jean Bonnin

Jean Bonnin was born in Lavaur, in the Tarn in France, in the year of the deep snows; he was brought up mainly in Wales and England. He took his first degree in government and politics at Birmingham, and his second in political philosophy at Hull; his doctoral research was on the theories of despotism. After university he lived and worked in France, Portugal, Ireland, and the former East Germany. On deciding to leave the underground and avant-garde music scenes of Berlin and northern France behind him – but not to abandon his music-making altogether – he returned to Wales where he now lives with his wife and his imaginary pelican.

Lines Within the Circle
An Original Publication of Red Egg Publishing

An imprint of Red Egg International
First published in the UK by Red Egg Publishing
in 2011

www.redeggpublishing.com

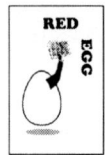

Copyright © Jean Bonnin 2011

Jean Bonnin has asserted his moral right to be identified as the author of this book.
Cover design: A. N. Griffiths and J. Bonnin

British Library Cataloguing-in-Publication Data
A catalogue record for this book is available upon
request from the British Library
ISBN: 978-0-9571258-0-3

While every effort has been made to contact copyright-holders,
if an acknowledgement has been overlooked, please contact the publisher

This book is sold subject to the condition that it shall not, by
way of trade or otherwise, be lent, re-sold, hired out, or otherwise
circulated without the publisher's prior consent in any form of
binding or cover other than that in which it is published and
without a similar condition including this condition being
imposed on the subsequent purchaser

Lines Within the Circle

A NOVEL BY

JEAN BONNIN

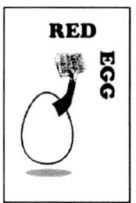

"A story should have a beginning, a middle, and an end… but not necessarily in that order."

Jean-Luc Godard

"Fortunately, somewhere between chance and mystery lies imagination, the only thing that protects our freedom, despite the fact that people keep trying to reduce it or kill it off altogether."

Luis Buñuel

CONTENTS

Quotes   6

Contents Page   7

Prologue   9

Main Section   11

Glossary   192

Notes and Acknowledgements   203

Prologue

I feel, I feel, I feel – I do feel... I feel like the invisible man who has surreptitiously entered an invisible man look-a-like competition and come third. Or, or, or possibly I am similar to the chess Grand Master Vyacheslav Rozhetskin who once took forty-five minutes before making his opening move.

Oh, I dunno... fuzzy-felt and all that. I guess it's simply that one has to live by one's decisions – or die by them, for that matter... I'd made my decision; and despite my frostbitten doubts, I knew that there was no turning... no 'U' turning... no, no turning back.

I

Everybody looked like corpses – distinguished, urbane, and smugly self-satisfied with their own demise. I could see the blue-lipped and waxen pallor death-stare of a very attractive Oriental woman through the gap between the seats opposite me. The train compartment's automatic door slid open and held itself patiently for several seconds before closing again. The woman, who looked disturbingly like Evi Ling, an ex from two years before, hadn't twitched a muscle. But then, as the train swung around a corner her head flopped to one side against the window, gently slid backwards, and rested between the curtain and the headrest.

It was a pity she was dead, I thought to myself. I would have liked to have questioned her to establish if she really was my ex lover… The man with the natty briefcase across the aisle from me looked like a demiurge for contemporary times, with a crown of thorns, navy blue suit, and a blue and white-striped tie splattered with droplets of blood.

With the sun on water outside my moving windowpane I realised I was the only one alive. I looked around me, through the window and up and down the carriage. On this helter-skelter planet of mine, at last I was alone and free – emerging slowly from under the waters of fellow beings who'd been breathing their claustrophobia directly into my lungs for so long. With their lips clamped tightly around my nose, and with a duck-taped mouth, they had blown their attitudes and impressions into me. And there had been no space for my self, for my survival, for my *own* attitudes…

But everybody was dead now – the whole world – and as a result I would be able to live longer. Longer, much much longer… much longer than you could shake a stick at the circling crows.

The train swooped around a corner like a dark angel, the demitasse of coffee I'd been holding spilt onto my crotch, and I awoke. I slowly looked around and grasped that, just as a dream can be the inverse of what some laughingly call reality, everybody was not dead. And possibly it was I who was dancing with ghosts.

II

Still not fully awake, and with no one in my carriage, I blurrily checked my reflection in the mirror that was at the base of a plastic camping cup that could be concertinaed down flat for easy storage. It was some little souvenir I'd picked up somewhere on my travels... My ear-length black hair, with its swept to the side off-centre parting, and floppy fringe that fell a little over my eyes if I didn't brush it to one side, looked lank. My nose was sharp and looked stern. My jaw was the shape of a chisel-toed Italian boot, and my cheeks protruded just enough to make me look interesting. My skin was paler than normal, and my eyes were slightly set back into my skull and had a dark haunted look to them. Under normal circumstances I gave myself between a seven and an eight out of ten. But since I hadn't been eating well, and my sleep patterns had been erratic for weeks, due to the worry as much as anything else I suppose, I appeared tired and exsanguinous, and thought it better to forget about my point system for the time being.

    I stood up and as I did so I caught my full-length double-glazed counterpart in the window as the train hurtled passed a disused warehouse. My black jeans looked grey, and I saw that I'd buttoned my blue jacket right up, although I couldn't remember when I'd done this. Reluctantly I stole my curious eye away from the perplexing image of the 5 feet 11 inches thin stranger gaping back at me, and took the remnants of my coffee and stood in the corridor...

    There I remained. And all the while, all the very long while, I watched as the outskirts of London became the inner-skirts.

The announcer announced that we would soon be arriving at our destination... I hadn't been to London for a long time – I had had no reason to. And in any case, on and off I'd been out of the country for several years... I let the other passengers get off first, before heaving my rucksack down the steps and onto the platform. With a tug and a swing I threw the deadweight over my shoulder and onto my back.

I slowly made my way towards the barrier, occasionally giving a twist or a wriggle in an attempt to even out the weight on my back. The hordes of homeward bound, outward-bound, city-bound, suburb lost and found, homeward bound dwellers rushed by and beyond me... Fingering inside my right trouser pocket I could feel the stiffness of the card that was my ticket; I scooped it out along with some coins of mixed denomination. One of the coins curved its way along the platform and over the edge down onto the track. The other four or five silver and copper coloured pieces lay lifelessly scattered at my feet.

The woman who looked like Evi Ling bent down like only a lady of breeding could, picked up my dropped coins and placed them with delicate precision into my palm. She smiled, turned, and headed towards the ticket barrier, and I watched her in her tight flower-print trousers as her bottom gave a slight bounce with each step that she took...

It was a gloomy day in the capital – all drizzle and hopelessness... I made my way to the station's internal café to gather my thoughts and my courage. I can no longer remember what it was called now – although I'm certain it was not so long ago. But I think it was something along the lines of The Traveller's Rest or The Happy Commuter, or some such oxymoron.

I sat down at one of the outside tables. Not really *outside* outside, since it was still inside the station and hence under its great Victorian roof; yet at least it was outside of the fake pub interior. When the waiter arrived to clear away the remains of the previous 'well-rested' traveller – a half-eaten Danish pastry and a cappuccino by the looks of the chocolate shavings that were clinging to the slowly solidifying froth – I ordered an espresso and lit a cigarette.

------•••------

I had once had the idea of writing a novel. A novel that conveyed the beautiful haphazardness of it all: the fact that we only happen to be where we are at any given moment because X, Y, and Z occurred, and equally because A, B, and C did not occur.

I mean to think, we are only with the partner we are with because we were in a certain bar at a certain time, for example. Had we been in another bar, or on another bus, or walking down a different road – because it had been raining, or because the phone had just rung as we were leaving the house, or we had met an old friend whilst walking down the road who only happened to be there at that time because someone had phoned *him* just before he was leaving – we would never have met the partner or person who was to change the course of our lives forever.

By the same token, if A, B, and C had occurred we may well have met some other person who would have changed our path forever. And we would never have known about the potential partner, friend, enemy, life-changer, sitting alone in some bar that we never quite made it to… But A, B, and C didn't happen; X, Y, and Z did…

At any moment in time, there are an infinite number of potential parallel realities, and we cannot go back and see what might have been. Oh, but if we could…

But I never did… write that novel, I mean.

------•••------

I took the remnants of my coffee and stood in the passageway. I stared out of the window, watching as the leafy suburbs of *Das Kapital*… no, no… um… watching as the leafy suburbs of *the capital* transformed into the dense greyness of traffic jams and garden-less housing. The voice crackled that we would soon be arriving at our destination, and we should ensure that we had all of our belongings with us. I had not been to London for a long time; I'd had no reason to – until now.

The train eventually scraped its way to a jerky standstill. I pulled the window down and stuck my hand out to turn the door handle. I left my rucksack propped against the doorframe as I descended onto the platform; then I reached back and bumped it down a step. It was heavy and I felt weak. I'd brought so much stuff – all rammed into that army surplus rucksack of mine. And, what was the point... what *really* was the point?

I eased my arms one by one through the straps and lumbered my bag onto my back. The queue of passengers impatiently waited until I'd got out of their way. They were twitchy and grimacing, and all of them undoubtedly had imperative things they had to be getting on with.

As I accepted their passing tuts and frowns with a quizzical smile, a vision of Oriental loveliness bobbed its way passed me along the platform. She was wearing tight flower-print slacks, oversized un-tucked white granddaddy shirt, a fraying blue denim jacket, and a smile for no apparent reason and directed at nothing in particular. A smile that was nevertheless distinctive for it rose out of a sea of scowls. She looked disconcertingly like someone with whom I had had an intense three-month fling several years before. I think she saw me gazing at her longingly – wishing I had time, or wishing this was another time... Or, maybe she just noticed me struggling with my rucksack.

III

It was from the dying embers of a particularly dry Portuguese summer, through till the end of that year that Evi Ling and I had been involved with each other.

I was living across the river from Porto in the town of Vila Nova de Gaia. It was a dusty old place with not much going for it except that it was across the river from Porto. Even the wine cellars, which were situated on the Vila Nova de Gaia side of the river, did not contain bottles of 'Gaia' but bottles of Port, much to the annoyance of the locals. But, in truth, there was beauty and charm on *both* sides of the river. A sublime beauty, which could most vividly be appreciated from the sixty-meter high upper tier, of the two-tiered, Ponte Dom Luís Bridge.

The banks of the river were steep and high. The precariously perched shanty shacks were colourfully painted in those southern-European-cum-north-African shades. And the innumerable washing lines that zigzagged their way down to the ancient minotaurian passageways below were strewn with flapping sheets and brightly coloured clothing.

Evi Ling lived in Corvilhã, a University town at the base of the Serra d'Estrella Mountains. She was teaching in one of Telford School's minor branches. I had first met her on the day of her arrival in Portugal. She had come to Telford School's main centre in Vila Nova de Gaia, where I was teaching. All new teachers had to come to HQ to meet the Principal and be allotted their particular outpost on the Portuguese map. Some poor souls, who had come south for sunshine and nightlife, found themselves teaching in schools where they were the only teacher in a small town with only two bars in it. And they had to spend more of a meditative year than they had hoped for.

------•••------

I can still feel the Portuguese warmth on my face – but it seems so distant now… everything does. Maybe I am the Sandyman – but in negative. Underexposed, overexposed – watching the colours fade in their cinematic fluids. Fluids draining and revealing, and I don't think I want to watch another film… on set, offset – Sandyman, dandyman, dada-man, gaga-man. Yah-yah man sitting in a tin can, spinning round for all he can. And turn the lights down low and be prepared for the beginning of the show – how now brown sow… stick the needle in the sacred cow… Oh yes, I think so – don't you?

Aaarrgghhh – beep beep, beep beep, beep beep yeah. Phew, foo, flew, flew-foo – flew over the jackdoor's home… Maybe I'm a tree swaying gently in the breeze. Trees and breeze, and sneeze – in a tight squeeze. Yeah a tree, yeah yeah yeah – that's it. Like in school, fool's gold; sold to the man in the snowshoes – yeah, like in school, in gym or drama or tree-class, hee! hee!... In school when the teach' said, hey pretend to be a tree swaying in the wind. Wind-turbines and snorting lines – going roun' 'n' roun' – oooo baby, lost and foun'. And yeah… the low-light sound emanating from the ground… or no, maybe yeah, from all around. Crackle to the buzz-whip and neck-lash – but still though, oh so still though……. No no no – that's not it. So, yeah – I remember there was a time when I'd wanted to write a book………………Un livre, ein buch. Yeah, thoughts are crazy whiplash moments of unfiltered desire. A book he said… the scream of the butterfly, he said… oh, read motherfucker read………………… No no no, yeah… OK now… Now!

Anyway, in logarithms 2+2=3.999 recurring… Anyway, anyhow, anywhere… um, I think that was a The Who song. No but… anyway, time's getting on I guess, and… and… and… yeah, so, what happened next? …

------•••------

IV

I had seen the job advertised in the newspaper: *Telford School of English. Vila Nova de Gaia, Portugal. Native English speaker required to teach a variety of levels and a variety of ages. Pay negotiable depending on age and experience...*

I sent them my Curriculum Vitae. And six or seven days after posting it I was phoned back on Thursday afternoon and told that if I wanted it the job was mine... I packed my black BMW - E21 - 316 to bursting point and set off from Ilford Road, Oxford, at 4 o'clock the following Monday morning. I had a week before classes started.

I had enjoyed my time in Oxford with its spires, gargoyles, and dons. And although I'd only been there for the duration of the summer on this occasion, it was time to move on: too many broken dreams, too many broken bicycles...

I crossed from Newhaven to Dieppe. I spent almost the entire four-hour crossing on the deck enjoying the late summer sun... I'd taken a map with me from the car, and spent some of the time planning my route. I wanted to avoid the French motorways, preferring the idea of descending leisurely through the gradually changing countryside. For the rest of the time, bar an occasional trip to the bar, I read my newly acquired novel purchased from Blackwell Bookshop a few days before.

I remember that the novel was set in some indeterminate time on planet earth. The world had been divided into two approximately equal parts. Equal in landmass, and in that neither had a monopoly over particular types of climate. It was not exactly fifty-fifty, but one part didn't exclusively have most of the temperate climates and luscious vegetation, while leaving the other with the barren lands and the unbearable heat.

This division had come about because greater Beings than us Earthlings, from some distant galaxy, had apparently been watching us for thousands of years. Their lack of comprehension and disgust at how man treated his fellow man led their leaders to send down representatives to Earth. And the first thing they did was to broadcast their message to the world simultaneously on all the television stations and radio stations.

This broadcast lasted for three days without cessation, in all the languages in which man still communicated. And, due to an inexperienced researcher at the recently expanded 'Planetary Library 10,000', in several languages that had long since died out – such as some of the native North American tongues, and Manx.

Their message explained who they were and where they were from – not that this meant anything to anyone. They told of their dismay at our stupidity and our cruelty, and that they could ignore it no longer. They were going to give us – the inhabitants of planet Earth – five weeks to end all wars. Five weeks to end all wars for good. And they said that they would return after our time had elapsed, either to congratulate us on our achievement, or to destroy our world.

Then towards the end of the broadcast the tone changed; from being stern, they almost became apologetic. They admitted that what they had seen had not been all bad: they were particularly fond of Black Adder, the first series; and apparently unicycles made them laugh a lot too. Nevertheless, these were but small flowers in a much larger sea of mud.

This was our last chance and, in the opinion of the extraterrestrial who was relaying his planet's message to us, they had given us more than enough time to achieve ever-lasting peace. Some of their ruling council, the Being on our televisions told us as an aside, had thought that thirteen hours and twenty-two minutes would have easily been sufficient to end all wars forever...

And that was that – with a 'good luck', and some kind of salute or a wave he, she, or it, faded into black and white buzzing particles, and then these particles got smaller and smaller until they disappeared completely from our screens. And after fifteen seconds the message started over... And surprisingly there was not a War of the Worlds type of panic, as you might have expected.

The religions of the world at first were rather flummoxed. Shortly though, they were able to re-interpret their Bibles or Korans or whatever it happened to be, and found some paragraph or other that had predicted the arrival of the aliens all along... While others pointed out that Nostradamus had not only predicted all of these extraterrestrial goings-on, he had got the date and time of their arrival spot on as well. But oddly, it was only after the aliens had come and gone that people were able to see all of this in Nostradamus' quatrains.

Presidents phoned Presidents, and Prime Ministers phoned their wives. Jason Tobias, Britain's first black PM flew to Washington, as did the Chairman of the Chinese Communist Party, as did the Russian leader, as did Fidel Castro's grandson – along with the French President, the German Chancellor, and most of the leaders of the world.

Three and a half weeks they spent negotiating, discussing, and arguing. It was a hell of a task. Not only were leaders of countries at these meetings, but also some of the most prominent freedom fighters, and terrorists. For, not only did wars between nations have to stop, but all fighting everywhere: internal conflicts and civil wars had to be resolved, as did all territorial disputes.

The leaders gave it, if not their best shot, a good shot. But there was too much bad blood between some of them; too much water had passed under the bloody flowing bridge. And it was difficult for certain parties to simply forget massacres, fixed election results, tortures, and beatings in the name of justice.

In the last week prior to the alien's promised return, people who lived apart from their loved ones began returning home. They wished to spend what they expected to be their last few hours together... And then as the time approached, the world sat in front of screens and around radios waiting for the end to be announced.

When he reappeared, 'Big Other' – as the press had nicknamed him – was very upset. Many of the wars *had* stopped, and a large number of the warring factions were on ceasefire. Even so, even with the number of conflicts in the world having been reduced by nearly seventy percent, guns were still being fired in anger... Nevertheless, he stated that since they were not destructive creatures, they would not be able to destroy our world after all. Instead, they would just reorganise it.

As far as Big Other could see, the great majority of sadness and conflict derived from wealth, or lack of it. And because of this they had decided to separate the world into two distinct systems: Market forces with no state intervention whatsoever – Capitalism in its purest form – would dominate one half; while the other half would be a form of Socialist society, where people would be looked after from cradle to grave. There would be no great inequalities in wealth, no private property, and innovation would not be greatly rewarded.

People would be allowed to change from one side to the other twice in their lives. If they were born on the Socialist side, for example, they could go over to the Capitalist side if they got fed up. If, however, they ended up hating the side they'd changed to, they could return to where they came from – but then that would be it for life; no more changes.

After the initial burst, the book lost its overtly science fiction leanings and proceeded to recount the lives of Daniel and Maria, who'd been born on either side of the divide... Daniel, bored and curious, crossed over. There he met and fell in love with Maria. Everything went smoothly until Maria made her intentions known to him, about wishing to leave for the other side.

The story recounted the turmoil this created for both of them. Especially for Daniel, who knew what he would be going back to if he followed Maria; and it would be his last permitted change from one side to the other, whereas Maria would still be able to return. Daniel attempts to explain the disadvantages of the other side to Maria, hoping to dissuade her from leaving. Yet, he perfectly understands the dislike she has for her birthplace, and her curiosity to discover the unknown.

Eventually the tearful separation is upon them. They agree however that if she has not returned to him within two years, he will make his final passage to go and join her. Since there is no contact allowed between the two sides, if she is not back by the end of the second year he will assume that she likes it where she is; and that she wishes them to spend the rest of their days together on that side… But two years is a long time, and a lot of things change in two years.

In a slightly haphazard fashion, everything does get resolved. There is even a final appearance from Big Other, who returns to Earth again hundreds of years later to assess whether everlasting peace has finally been achieved, and if people are happier under this new arrangement than they had been under the old world order.

It wasn't a long story – maybe sixty or seventy pages. And as I finished the last sentence and closed the book, I got up from where I'd been sitting and saw France pulling towards me…

------•••------

This was a book though, a detail. Only a detail. That's all it was – a book; nothing more than that. And I mustn't get distracted, sidetracked, waylaid. Details can be interesting, but that's not the point. Point… pointy point – point to point, heel to toe… with my feet in the snow. No! My life – a certain part of my life – is the but du jeu.

I suppose I could have started whenever I liked – I mean, I could have begun with my childhood, but… I dunno – for whatever, yeah whatever, reason I've begun with the not too distant past. Maybe a past that led to the present… But all that has past leads to the here and now. And possibly I will always be able to remember these days, and there's no rush at all. But it's a pleasant exercise remembering all of these not too far away shenanigans; though they do seem that much further now. I wonder why that is?

But this is all swivelling away from my given path. I will stay focused. And I will keep thinking about all of this. It is a good exercise in itself. But more than that, it is necessary.

I did once consider writing a book, books... a book. Yeah, something like that. It was vaguely gonna be about someone who was either mad or immortal... possibly both. I can't remember any longer. I never... no no, never got around to it. Possibly being published would have been a way of manifesting my own immortality. If you're published... I mean to say if you're published you're always published. Your name is always on that spine – long after your own spine has withered into ashes... ashes. Ashes to ashes, funk to funky – we know Major Tom's a junky. Yeah – all of that...

But I must concentrate... concentrate on the task at hand.

------•••------

V

I got off the boat to a warm sunny day with swirls of clouds in a watercolour sky... About an hour from Dieppe I stopped in a small town to refuel and stock up on cigarettes. I pulled into the service station of a giant supermarket called *Mammouth*. I filled up the tank and gave the windows a wipe with a yellow sponge, which had been left in a soapy bucket of graying liquid.

I bought a baguette, a wedge of Brie, a bottle of red wine, and a bottle of sparkling water from the supermarket. Once back at the car I opened the doors to let the heat out, and went to sit on a small grassy knoll near the parking lot to eat the Brie and baguette sandwich I was about to make, and have a few swigs of the cheap red I'd just bought.

A cavalcade passed by, at the centre of which was a chauffeured open-topped black limousine with a couple sitting on the back seat. I heard a loud bang, or maybe it was two or three – I forget now. I paid little attention to the backfiring jalopy with the Dallas number plate however, and continued with my lunch. And after fifteen minutes I was ready to set off again.

The luscious rolling Normandy countryside gave way to long straight tree-lined roads, and eventually to vineyards. The sun shone, the window was open, the driving was not fast but steady, and the Cocteau Twins I was playing on my car stereo suited the landscape somehow.

As I descended through the country the houses began to be painted in brighter colours, the roofs became flatter, and palm trees began to replace what had been apple trees at first, and then vines. The earth became redder, yellowier, and more sandy. And the language, like the lifestyle, became slower and more relaxed. Less harsh, less abrupt, more drawn out, more 'what's the rush?'.

After driving for over eight hours, with only an occasional stop for coffee or petrol, the bright moon signalled the end of the day… I parked up in a service station's parking area for the night. Almost as soon as I'd let the seat down and got comfortable in my sleeping bag, I fell asleep. I was tired and slept well for the most part.

My only slight disturbance was a dream I had about my uncle. He'd been a scientist doing supposedly groundbreaking work; but since it was all a little hush-hush, I was never privy to the details. We didn't see each other that often, once every few years at a family Christmas get-together, for example. This was a pity because when we did see each other we got on really well.

But he'd sadly died the previous year. And about six weeks after his death I'd received an envelope with a key in it. The key was to a safe-deposit box. It had taken me another six or seven weeks before I'd got around to going up to London to see what mysterious thing my uncle had left me. Feeling like a spy in an alcove, I'd opened the package in the basement of the bank. I didn't look at the contents in detail at that time – that only came later. But on giving the papers – for that's all the package contained – a rudimentary glance, it looked like they mainly contained formulae and equations. On the last page, however, in my uncle's handwriting was a brief letter. At the bottom of the page, in large letters, underlined, were the words: *If in trouble phone this number…* followed by a phone number.

And this in its mixed up manner was the content of my dream. The difference between what had occurred in reality and my dream, was that in my dream there were sinister looking characters skulking around corners and in alleyways; and as I'd made my way through the streets of London, and back to the station to catch my train home, I was constantly aware of being watched…

In the morning I washed, shaved, and cleaned my teeth in the café's toilets. Then I bought three croissants and a coffee, and went and sat at an outside table in the rising early morning sun.

Soon after leaving, the southern French smells and sounds transformed into the dusty barren lands of northern Spain. No longer slowed down by passport controls I whizzed across the border into a land completely new to me. If it had not been for the word 'España' written on the blue EU sign with its circle of yellow stars, I wouldn't have known I'd crossed into another country.

Shortly after crossing into Spain, I spotted a sign by the roadside stating that the Salvador Dali Museum was only ten kilometres away. And coincidentally, a little after turning off the highway a Tangerine Dream track started playing from my compilation tape… And I recall how the music, coupled with my arrival in Figueras, the little town where the Dali museum was located, reminded me of something I'd read whilst in Oxford:

In 1965, in the Catalonian town of Cadaqués, Edgar Froese met Salvador Dalí. A meeting that was to change Edgar's life forever… He eventually returned to West Berlin stating that what Dali created in painting he wanted to create in music. "This was the biggest change I ever had in music. By seeing the way he was talking and thinking, I found that everything was possible. I thought that I would do the same thing as he did in painting in music," he later said. And that was how the idea for the group that eventually became known as Tangerine Dream came about…

The Dali museum's roof had giant white eggs sitting on tall towers. And the inside also lived up to what one hoped for from the gallery of the high priest of dream reality… A great table-less banqueting hall adorned with immense canvases of moments between sleep and wake, caught and caressed into our waking world, was at the far end of the building. As spiral staircases wound up to passages on three floors.

To the front of the hall was a large opening surrounded by grotesquely oversized archers' alcoves in which were subtly stained cathedral windows. Looking out through these windows, or through the openings in the wall, you gazed down upon a central courtyard: the surrealist's inner courtyard, which was sheltered from the elements by a glass dome.

In this inner courtyard, next to a fountain, was the second black limousine of my journey. Inside this one were four dummies with violins in their hands. It was raining on the dummies – from inside the limousine. And from a loud speaker hidden somewhere within the car came the screeching sound of disorder. I remember thinking that the sound could have been played by some strange minstrel quartet at the feasting table for the King of Mars.

On the second floor, in a dimly lit room covered with blood-red flock wallpaper was a stepladder. Facing the ladder on the far side of the room was a crimson-coloured lip-shaped sofa. When you climbed to the top of the ladder and looked through the 'viewing box', you saw the face of a woman. The sofa made up the mouth, the lamps behind the sofa made up the nostrils and nose. Two previously rather non-descript wall hangings above the nose – once looked at through this 'distortion box' – made up the eyes and lashes. And on the inside of the box was the hair and outline of a chin. The complete effect, which was only obvious once observed through this convex viewing-glass, was one of a woman's face with a rather voluptuous mouth.

I took a photograph of this optical illusion, which I later framed; and which later still, I would place on my desk – whatever desk, and wherever that happened to be. I do not know why really, maybe simply because I liked the photograph so much. Or maybe there was a deeper meaning... as... as... so many things seem now to have.

I walked past the dummy-screeches coming from the black limousine, out and up to my parking spot; and with one final stare into the egg I was off again...

After the Dali museum I headed down the coast, and spent two nights in Barcelona. I found a surprisingly cheap – 'surprising' considering its location – shabby room in a guesthouse in Las Ramblas.

My first day in the Catalonian capital was spent on the track of Antoni Gaudí – traversing the city from Metro to bus, and from tapas bar to tapas bar. His park, *Parc Güell*, was quirky and colourful – with its hallucinatory hues, twisted columns, amorphous shapes, and giant amphibians. And I spent a happy couple of hours wandering around there, and then sitting at a stone table to eat my bread and cheese.

However, his *Temple Expiatiori de la Sagrada Familia*, with its one hundred meter mutated towers, I found to be horrendous. Admittedly it was impressive – especially when I considered the years and years that Gaudí had spent living in a little hut on site. But to me it was a monolithic monstrosity depicting some apocalyptic vision, created by a very dark mind... I was aware that mine was not a popularly held opinion. But I remember feeling vindicated when months later I read that George Orwell had also hated it.

I can no longer call to mind what I did the following day... but I have a vague memory of dancing with a Spanish woman wearing a brown and rusty red flowing dress. Somewhere... somewhere... possibly in a cellar bar – I don't know. She had ringlets of hair that bounced along with her swaying motions. And I do remember feeling happy. That I remember – the *feeling* I remember well. But that is all. For the time being that is all...

I was up early on the day of my departure; I had to be out of my guesthouse by ten o'clock. I figured I could drive quite a way before lunch, and then hopefully reach Portugal by nightfall.

I recall that as I drove steadily along the slab of tarmac heading westwards, my mind began to find its own pace. And I remember my thoughts drifting back over the time I had just spent in Oxford...

During that first stint of mine in Oxford, prior to my departure for the sun and a Portuguese view of life, I discovered a little out of the way film theatre that specialised in foreign language films. On those drizzly middle England days when the puddles would splash you, and the rainwater would spurt up your trouser legs as you cycled by, I would shelter from those long grey afternoons that contained no hint of irony, watching hour upon hour of French films...

I hadn't known anything about the films made by *La Nouvelle Vague* when I'd first been enticed into that cinema. A poster on the wall outside the cinema had announced the beginning of a *Nouvelle Vague* season. And after watching 'Le Dernier Métro' by François Truffault on that first evening – which was admittedly a late Truffault film – the following day I'd gone to the library to find out as much as I could about the genre.

And as far as I remember it was this that dominated my thoughts as the Spanish road peeled backwards underneath my car, and the landmarks in my rearview mirror became further away until they gradually transformed into my past...

La Nouvelle Vague – was a term coined to define the sudden influx of new talent into the French cinema between 1958-1960, when 67 new directors embarked on their first feature films.

At the forefront of this movement was the *Cahiers de Cinéma* group of critics – François Truffault, Jean-Luc Goddard, Claude Chabrol, Eric Rohmer, and Jacques Rivette, for example.

The commercial and artistic success of their first films, made very quickly, cheaply, and without established stars, revolutionised production in the French film industry. *La Nouvelle Vague* in essence was a reaction to the Hollywood-style films that had gone before. The big budget American movies that were 'artificially' made in studios, with back-projection and dubbed on sound, were seen by this group of new directors as being passé; one-dimensional entertainment with very little artistic or cultural value.

Even though the improvisation, hand-held cameras, location shooting, and minimal technical crews of these new directors was at least as much to do with economy as principle, they were nevertheless trying to create realism in cinema. I suppose in a similar way to how I'm attempting to re-create the 'real' from my own cinema of flickering thoughts...

This cinematic revolution of theirs could not have been possible without the parallel emergence of new film technology, such as the hand-held camera. For what is more *real* than a hand-held camera following someone in the street; being in close proximity to their expressions and emotions, with the sound of people's everyday lives resonating throughout?

------•••------

Who said that?

------•••------

In this sense then, along with the often improvisational nature of the action and reaction in the early *Nouvelle Vague* films, some of the films could almost be seen as documentary in style. Maybe fly-on-the-wall is going a little too far, but you often had an overwhelming feeling that you were indeed watching someone's life in motion…

As I drove through the sunlight I recollect thinking about an article I'd read whilst in Oxford, written by Alexandre Astrue in 1948. He wrote something along the lines of how directors should manipulate their art in the same manner as writers employ the written word. He stated that cinema should be as subtle and flexible as the words on a page. He called this approach the *caméra-stylo*. And, for Truffault, this meant directly using literature, art, and culture, in his films. Almost, it seemed, with the intention of educating his audience…

The great paradox however, of the *Nouvelle Vague*'s thrust for 'authenticity', was that despite using unknowns in their films, once the films became successes the by-product was that these films had themselves created 'stars'. But unfortunately, there appeared to be no way around this…

And now that I come to think about all this, I seem to recall that my copy of Jean-Paul Sartre's book *Nausea* opened with a sentence along the lines of: "Maybe I should write down everything that I say and do…" And, for me, there was an element of this form of existentialism that ran through the early *Nouvelle Vague* films…

------•••------

The struggle in my mind between a blurred state of numbness and an uncannily precise recollection of snippets from my life, at times produces confusion; and at other times, I see them as intriguing asides that keep me from getting bored...

My brain seems to want to spurt out facts to me. Spuriously disguised as being relevant to the tale I wish to recount... to recount... to recount – to recall. But this is not the time for quiz machine trivialities. This is the time, for it is definitely inextricably related to time... this is the time when I wish to retrace all that has gone before. All that has gone before, for me. Only me. Yet, not all *either. Just that which has led up to this.*

I believe it will help in some way. Maybe it won't. But maybe it will. And anyway, it is all I have. And my life – my immediate life – is important to me. It is who I am, who I was... and... and... and – who I will become.

Before I clean my teeth, I always ensure that the last flavour in my mouth is a pleasurable one... The last thing I eat from my Christmas dinner plate is never an invariably forgettable sprout; it is always a succulent slither of turkey, which I have purposefully left until the very end...

------•••------

I allowed Barcelona to evaporate in my rear-view mirror. The driving, on a road that stretched out into the horizon, was trance inducing. My music cassette had stopped over thirty minutes earlier, and once I finally became aware of this, I fingered my cassette boxes that were piled on my passenger seat. I was looking for one I had put together on a rainy day in Oxford. It had a multi-coloured deck-chair style cover that I had cut out and made from a magazine ad.

After a couple of minutes of rooting around while intermittently flitting my gaze to and from the road in front, I found the tape. I fast-forwarded and rewound it until I found the track I was looking for. And although it was little more than a pop song, it was nevertheless the song sung by the French actress Jeanne Moreau in Truffault's film *Jules et Jim*... I'd wanted to find the song, 'Le Tourbillon', I remember, because it seemed an appropriate conclusion to my line of thinking.

…As the song was coming to an end I pulled onto a slip road that led to a service station and cafeteria. It was lunchtime, and I needed sustenance…

I shuffled my tray along the metal rungs. It was shortly before midday and a wide selection of hot and cold food was on offer. I settled for a just-out-of-the-oven-and-placed-under-the-bright-serving-lights slice of Spanish omelette, bread, coffee, and a glass of water. I waited at the cash register for two or three minutes while the till woman finished off her conversation with a colleague the other side of the serving hatch.

From being alone, by the time she returned to take my money, there were three people patiently waiting behind me. I turned around from facing the counter to discreetly steal a glimpse of my fellow brunchers… The young woman standing just behind me had a coffee and what looked like a strawberry cheesecake on her tray. I estimated she was in her mid-twenties, and no taller than 5 ft 5 ins. On that first sideways glance in her direction – pretending that I was looking over her head at the menu board – I had thought she had a hair lip. But when I looked again a few moments later, I realised that the corner of her upper lip had merely rolled under and stuck on what must have been her dry gums.

Her hair was as white as the 'furnishings' in a Nordic ice-hotel and, in the 'Is she?/Isn't she?' classic list of hair terminology, was probably 'fly-away'. At least that is what its wispy directionless nature suggested to me… She was very pretty in what I thought was a fragile, porcelain, china doll kind of way; and was perfect in her compactness. She wore black jeans and dark blue T-shirt. I think – I think I thought – that her lip might have got caught whilst trying to smile in my direction. But possibly the wish was the father of the thought, in this instance. I did not look again. The cashier took my money and gave me my change in a starchily efficient manner.

I sat down by the window; then I quickly changed my seat to sit the opposite side of the table so that the sun was no longer in my eyes. I unloaded the contents of the tray on the table, and then placed the tray on the seat next to me. Crudely slicing away a piece of my omelette with my fork, spearing it and popping it in my mouth, I watched as an articulated lorry tried to reverse from an awkward angle into a narrow space between two other lorries. And I thought for a while about the word 'jack-knife'.

I had put too much tomato ketchup on my plate. I dipped and ate. I slipped my pocket world atlas out of my jacket pocket. I noted that if you were able to pick Portugal up from its Mediterranean bottom and let it drop 180° over its northern most point it would not quite reach Brest in western France; whereas, much more entertainingly, if you toppled Italy over it would reach Anglesey in north Wales – probably at the village with the very long place name. Nonetheless, I magnanimously decided not to be over-critical of Portugal's inability to reach anywhere amusing with my swivel test.

Looking at the Spain and Portugal page, I figured it would take me longer than I'd hoped to reach Portugal. And to reach Porto I reckoned it would take me at least a day, or day and a half. The route I had opted for would take me through the mountains where the roads were small. But it didn't matter; I had the time, and the weather was good.

As far as I could remember 'jack-knife' had three meanings: what must have been its original meaning, which was a knife that folds in on itself so that the blade goes into the handle; there was the jack-knife dive which is where the diver tucks himself in in mid flight, which I seem to remember is also known as the forward pike; and the lorry related definition that set this idle line of thinking off in the first place – where the cabin part of the lorry doubles round on itself and the whole thing goes out of control.

The white-haired woman had perched herself at the next table along, facing my way. The thick frame of the emergency exit door, which was situated between our two tables, allowed this woman with the sixteenth century smile to face the sun and yet remain in shadow. Her legs were crossed under the table. She had black clogs on, and one of her feet was twitching. She kept bouncing her crossed leg so that her clog would slip to the end of her foot, and just at the last moment as it was about to fall to the ground she would flick her big toe, shuffle and tilt her foot backwards. And the almost free footwear would return to its snug position obediently. When I realised that I'd been transfixed by this movement I quickly looked up.

She had caught me looking and gave me her Giaconda smile; in return I gave her a slightly affected bashful 'ooops, I was just staring at anything in my line of vision and not especially at your legs' look in return.

More or less sated I lit a cigarette and prepared to drink my coffee. Only after I had managed to squirt a thin stream of milk across the table though. It is the intrinsic design fault of these little plastic 'milk pods' that to some people make them quirky. And no doubt in thirty or forty years time, from the distorted memories of the future, they will be considered as design icons and will be looked back upon with fondness and a sense of nostalgia. It having all too easily been forgotten that these little things are in fact useless...

The coffee was strong and it gave me a lift; and I was ready for the next stint of my journey. I went to the toilet and filled up my water bottle from the cold tap. I then filled the car up with petrol. On my way back towards the main road I stopped to pick up the white-haired woman with the lop-sided smile, who was looking for a ride with her thumb raised skywards. She slung her bag onto the back seat, sat down, and shook my hand. She smelt of cigarettes and musky perfume. And her name was perfect: Slinky Klingerbeel.

She talked and I drove. She was a beguiling creature and instantly made herself at home by slipping her clogs off, reaching under her seat to slide the chair backwards, and putting her bare feet up on the dashboard. Her toenails were painted different colours: red, blue, green, purple, and silver. She had a silver bracelet around her right ankle. And her black eyeliner and general demeanour meant she had a slightly startled just-got-up-out-of-bed aura about her.

Slinky spasmodically gave a little head twitch, which rather than being some affected cutesy mannerism, or even a tic, I put down to the kind of flick of someone who used to have long hair. Her English could not be faulted, although occasionally, maybe with words that she did not often employ, a slight accent was detectable – sometimes coupled with the over emphasis of one syllable rather than another.

She was very at ease with herself and talked freely. She seemed happy to have someone to talk to, and unselfconsciously skipped from subject to subject. And I was content to do more of the listening…

VI

Slinky reached behind and produced a book from her bag. It was the book she had been reading on her travels – since flying from Reykjavik to Barcelona the previous week. It was a going away present from a friend who had seen her off at the airport. After having waved the cover in front of my face, she asked for a swig of water from my bottle, which was rolling around at her feet. And after gulping down a third of the bottle, she began recounting the story to me…

It was about a journalist-cum-writer in some totalitarian régime who was trying to inform people, via the means of his regular weekly column for a newspaper, about what was really going on under their oppressive system. It was a very fine line: the line between what the régime would permit, and the *truth*. And each week as he set about writing his piece he was never sure where that line was.

The thing that concerned him most was what would happen to him if he 'obviously' crossed the line… He spent many soul-searching hours figuring out how to phrase things in a certain way, with a certain use of language or a well chosen play on words, which would get him past the censors and thus published. And yet, he wanted those who read his articles, with a little delving between the lines, to understand the real message he was trying to convey.

Slinky opened her book, which she had been holding in her lap and took out a postcard. She held the card in her right hand and kept her place by inserting her index finger between the pages where the card had been. She read its inscription. She said they were the words of John Swainton, former Editor of the New York Times, addressing his staff on the day of his retirement:

"There is no such thing as a free press. You know it and I know it. There is not one of you who would dare to write his honest opinion. The business of a journalist is to destroy the truth, to lie outright, to pervert, to vilify, fall at the feet of mammon and sell himself for his daily bread. We are tools, vessels of rich men behind the scenes, we are jumping jacks. They pull the strings – we dance. Our talents, our possibilities and our lives are the properties of these men. We are intellectual prostitutes."

"I want to be a journalist," said Slinky. And then she threw her head back against the headrest and guffawed. "Anyway..." she said, and continued with her account of the novel:

As time goes on, so she told me, he feels progressively more frustrated with his inability to 'tell it how it is'; and step by little step he takes more and more, what he sees as necessary, risks.

At the same time as compiling his columns, he is writing a book. A book, which Slinky said, he becomes so absorbed with it becomes difficult to distinguish the fiction from the reality. And it gradually becomes less easy to distinguish between what he is writing and what he is living. You begin to wonder if what he is writing in his novel is in some bizarre way self-fulfilling.

He becomes increasingly obsessed with his book, and as he does so he becomes more reclusive... He is pushing himself to construct a novel about the life of a mind that is trying to write a book. It is sort of a circle within a circle within a circle, Slinky tells me.

After some time, he begins to have hallucinations, if indeed that's what they are. These 'visions' usually come to him at night, as he is sitting at his old oak writing table in his bed-sit on the fifth floor. And the visions are always of a cube of white light spinning towards him from the middle distance…

He spends his evenings sitting writing by the light of the light bulb on its long flex, which hangs just above his desk. And when he's not writing, and is lost in his introspections, staring out of his window over the slated roofs of the city, allowing his mind and eyes to focus on dreams and nothingness, he glimpses a speck. That's always how it starts, as a speck that vibrates towards him. And as it approaches, its form gradually becomes distinguishable. It is a small shimmering particle of white heat floating above the roofs and houses; and as it gets closer it transforms into a growing cuboid of whiteness. And steadily it undulates, sways, and hones in on him.

Then several hours after seeing the cube, he regains his senses, and comes to with his head slumped upon his folded arms. And on each separate occasion, long stretches of time have elapsed that he cannot account for; sometimes it is already morning.

On one occasion he awakes to a big black bird flapping outside his window in the spot where the last thing he remembers is the undulating box. And another time, he awakes to the light bulb swinging above his head and the four or five paragraphs he was convinced he had written prior to dozing off having disappeared.

Slinky reached forward and picked up the empty cassette box from the dashboard. She opened it up and started reading the track titles. "Which song is this?" she asked.

"'Sarah Sunshine' by The Living," I told her. She was clearly trying to find it written on the flap. "It's half way down the second side," I said.

"Oh yeah, I've got it," she said. "And it's followed by 'Dentist Drill' by Dogger Fisheur German Bite?"

"If that's what it says on the cover."

"…D'you want me to carry on?" she asked.

"Sorry?"

"With the book, I mean."

"Yes. I'm intrigued to know what happens at the end."

"Oh, I don't know how it ends 'cos I haven't finished it yet, but I can tell you as far as I'm up to."

She proceeded to tell me how on one occasion after the protagonist had spent several hours chatting and drinking homemade wine with the couple that lived in the flat next to him, he returned to sit at his desk and read over what he'd written earlier that evening. He read, although not fully concentrating, and he thought, with a smile on his face, about the conversation he had just had with Caroline and Stephanie.

(Apparently, the idea of gay and lesbian couples was actually encouraged. Not that the régime was in any way liberal-minded but because of the scarcity of resources – which was partly due to over-population.

It was reasoned that the more homosexual couples there were, the fewer new-borns there would be. And there were many financial benefits to be had from being in a long-term gay relationship. Indeed the State had more registered homosexuals per capita of the population than any other geo-political area in the world.

It must be emphasised that this society wasn't concerned with anything other than its own survival. It certainly wasn't interested in human rights. For example, voluntary castration or voluntary female sterilisation was strongly 'encouraged'.

Of the many registered gay couples that lived in this régime, many were heterosexuals who were pretending to be gay... Gay couples were left to their own devices much more than straight couples of a childbearing age. Frequently two straight couples would pair off – the two men would pretend to be together, and the two women would also act as if they were an item. And often the two women and two men would all become very close friends. Even to the extent that they would go out together in foursomes – acting normally when out [i.e. as though they were really in same sex relationships], but swapping back over once they were home).

Zaccariah – for now that I think about it I recall that was what Slinky said his name was – sat at his desk smiling. Smiling because of things they had been talking about, but also because he doubted whether Caroline and Stephanie were a lesbian couple at all. He could not quite put his finger on it, just little things really. Little things that all added up. Two single beds for example, although admittedly pushed together. And the way they were with each other once they had relaxed after a few glasses of wine.

The principal reason he was smiling was that if his hunch was correct it meant that his next-door neighbours were also acting against the State. And this meant that maybe he would have allies he could confide in.

"Shall I turn the tape over?" Slinky asked.

"D'you want to choose another one, that one's already been round once."

"I've got a tape in my bag, if..."

"Stick it on," I told her.

She rummaged around behind her on the back seat. After a couple of minutes of unsuccessful searching, she undid her seatbelt, knelt on her chair, and reached over to fish around in her holdall. After a short while, punctuated with the occasional sigh or tut, she turned back around with a pensive look on her face.

"Umm, that's odd," she said addressing herself as much as me.

"Can't find it?" I ventured, stating the obvious.

"Umm," she repeated, whilst staring out of the windscreen.

"Put one of those compilation tapes on with the stripy covers," I suggested.

"Got it," she announced.

I glanced to my left to see her triumphantly holding a tape aloft. She had finally found it in one of her jacket pockets. She popped it in the stereo, and it whirred into understated jazzy action.

"Where was I? Oh yeah… so Zaccariah was sitting thinking at his writing table… and it was raining. Did I say it was raining? Well, it doesn't really matter except that he stood up and reached over his desk to close his window."

I remember her telling me that as he stretched over to shut his window and pull the curtains, he once again saw the dazzlingly white block coming towards him. This time he decided to stay standing. With his thighs pressed against his desk and supporting himself with his out-stretched hands, he peered directly into its bright-light bright-white centre.

It kept coming, maybe quicker than before. He remained still. And at about fifty metres away, and seemingly the size of a garden shed, it stopped; it was still shuddering but not advancing. This had not happened before, or at least he had not been conscious to see it. He turned to look at the clock by his bed, but it must have stopped for it read three hours earlier than it should have been. He pulled the cord to turn the light off. And as the light clicked off he heard a burst of laughter coming from his next-door neighbours, which subsided into giggles and then was gone. Then suddenly he heard a whoosh of wind and momentarily he blanked out. And when his eyes reopened he found himself inside the box.

"The next chapter or so..." Slinky went on to tell me "is really strange. All about his experiences within his new white world; and within his head as well, really."

Slinky did not dwell too much on this part of the novel, saying that it was all about introspection and paranoia – as far as she could work out – and that I basically had to read it myself...

Eventually Zaccariah finds himself in a 'perfect' little world. Neatly cut lawns, blooming herbaceous borders, detached whitewashed houses with double-glazing, patios and double garages; and culs-de-sac where residents wave and smile on their way to work. And like the memories of the summers of our youth, the sun is always shinning.

Zaccariah is lost and distrusting; this is not his world... The last thing he remembers of his home is the white box coming towards him over the cityscape on that drizzly evening. And then he wakes up beside a beautiful woman that he has never seen before... And he gazes up at the ceiling like a ventriloquist's old wooden dummy, the scary kind, lifeless and with staring eyes.

Zaccariah and his wife Ulla live at 6 Liberty Drive. He has a shirt and trousers and a fluffy towel, and no longer a jumper with baggy elbows. Next door, to their right, live the Mandins, a French couple with snubby noses and a sausage for a dog. Monsieur Mandin likes tweed; Mme Mandin wears green gardening gloves when she kneels down to pull out uninvited guests. She has a slight moustache but since her hair is light in colour it is only detectable when close up. His moustache is dark brown, like the remaining tufts of hair on his thinning pate. It is thicker at the bottom than the top. Its progressive density, as one's gaze follows it down from its origins at the base of M. Mandin's nose towards his mouth, where it forms a little ridge above his lip, makes one think of a brush. He is far more cock-sure than the reality would merit; and he thinks he is a wow with the women.

Opposite number six are the Arrowsmiths, locally known as 'the couple with the spastic child'.

"Are you going to turn the alarm off darling?" enquires the well-spoken voice coming from the pillow to his left. The room is still sombre, although a ray of light has circumspectly burrowed its way between the blinds, bounced off the dressing–table mirror and is languishing on the face of the woman lying next to Zaccariah.

Zaccariah stirs and becomes aware of a high-pitched beeping coming from his right. He turns to see the outline of what must be a clock on the bedside cabinet; the red figures at its centre read 33:01. He reaches, feels, and with a groping index finger the thing is pacified. Having either switched it off or at least snoozed it, he slowly pulls the covers off him. He turns his bottom slightly so he can first lower his feet to the ground, and then edge himself gently into a sitting position on the side of the bed.

Deep breathing is now coming from the other side of the bed. He turns, looks at the stranger beside him, shakes his head, and turns back – and he hopes he is in a dream… He notices a socket with a plug in it; gently he pulls it out. And the red figures from the dark oblong clock-face disappear. Carefully, so as not to disturb the stranger next to him, he slowly stands up. And once again he turns – his gaze follows the line of sunlight up the woman's arm and onto her face... Who is this beautiful dark-haired stranger? he wonders.

Before making his way towards the two doors, which are in the wall opposite the king-size bed, he gathers himself enough to realise that it may be less suspicious if he plugs the clock back in. It momentarily flashes 00:00 before 33:01 reappears.

The nearest of the two doors is ajar. Anxious of what he'll find, he cautiously steps through. A strip-light above a bathroom mirror clicks on automatically. He looks at himself in the mirror. He looks pale, tired. He is wearing some chic black silk pyjamas with a circle on the breast pocket. Inside this circle is a vertical black semi-circle next to which are four parallel black lines of varying lengths. He sticks out his tongue, it is furry; he puts what looks like toothpaste and smells of mint onto his index finger and rubs his teeth. He turns the water on and rinses, using his cupped hands.

Behind him on the towel rack, which slopes out from the wall, are two sumptuous sky blue towels. On one is stitched the word Zac, and on the other Ulla... As quickly as he can, without making a noise, he leaves the shiny show-home bathroom. Through the second door he finds himself on a landing with a pine balustrade, that looks down onto an open-plan living room. To the left, at the end of the landing, is a spiral staircase.

He descends into the living room. And all the while he hopes he is in a dream, the strangest of dreams – caught between day and night, light and dark. And like the best dreams, it is like being trapped in a tableau of melting clocks, full of beautiful women and just-out-of-reach meanings. But something – possibly the lucidity of his thoughts, or the underlying feeling he has of being out-of-control – something... something is screaming to him that none of this resembles the comforting halfway-house of a dreamland.

He picks up the newspaper that has been left splayed and open over the eggshell powder blue and white striped settee. The date at the top is more or less the correct date; there is no year however. On flicking through the paper he sees that it is only a local rag. And as such, it contains nothing useful about his newly found perfect environment; nothing about what is going on in this world. Only garden fêtes, the building of a new swimming pool, and the proud announcement that one of their own had won a national writing prize for a piece about production.

Zaccariah goes over to the bookshelf. The shelves are made out of some unfamiliar looking metal – maybe it is titanium, but Zaccariah isn't sure. The shelves have two wooden poles that originate from two holes in the floorboards, which penetrate each metal shelf at either end. The shelves are as high as the room, with a ladder at one end, which is attached to the shelves with rollers. And the ladder is on castors so it can be pushed along to reach the books at either end.

The shelves are not parallel to the floor; each one slopes to a varying degree, from right to left, or left to right. However, since the bottom of the spine of each book has been cut to the appropriate angle, the books look upright. So, although each book may look horizontal at the top, they are all of differing lengths.

Zaccariah reads along some of the spines: 'Healthy Body Healthy Find'; 'Jazz with one Zed'; 'The History of History'; 'Journalism and the Accepted Truth'; 'Procreation, Continuation, Information'; 'Property and Proper Tea'; 'Ist, Ism, Y'; 'The Cubist's House'; 'Tombebouc'…

Behind Zaccariah in the far corner of the room is an archway with half-length wooden-panelled saloon-style swing doors. After tossing a glance up to the bedroom door on the landing, he makes his way across the room. He puts his hands on top of the two swing doors and peers through. More pastel colours greet him in what is clearly the kitchen. 'Clearly' because, apart from there being a sink, a stove, and what looks like a fridge, above the draining board are the letters T-H-E-K-I-T-C-H-E-N written in bold metallic-sheen orange. The wall on which it is written, as is the case with the whole kitchen, is apple green. Apart that is from the occasional square or oblong of colour painted in one of the corners of the room, or painted on the upper reaches of one of the walls and slightly over-lapping onto the ceiling.

He pushes through the swing doors and goes to open the fridge. He picks up a small round box from the bottom shelf that has 'The Cheese' written on its lid – underneath which is a circle, half black and half white, with four straight lines in the white half.

He tears off a chunk of the yellow oblong and pops it in his mouth. Disappointingly, he finds it to be virtually without any taste.

In the washing machine Zaccariah finds an oily pair of jeans and a black T-shirt. The black T-shirt looks crumpled, and yet when Zaccariah holds it up to his nose it has that shop-new aroma to it. He throws the pyjamas he'd woken up in into the washing machine. Zaccariah slips the jeans and T-shirt on. They both fit perfectly. On the mat by the kitchen's backdoor he sees two pairs of black plimsolls, one pair with a thin dark blue flash and the other with a tiny red flash. The blue ones are the larger of the two and also fit perfectly.

Through the glass in the kitchen door he sees that the back garden is a back garden – with a tree, a tall brown wooden fence, a wooden bench that for some reason is upside down, and one of those lawn mowers that you sit and drive around on.

At the other end of 'THE KITCHEN' is another door; Zaccariah turns the key in the lock and goes through. He is at the top of four steps that lead into a car-less garage. If not a double garage it is at least a 'one-and-a-half' garage. The shelves that line two and a half of the walls are filled with items you'd expect to find in a garage: nails, oil, spanners of various shapes and sizes, hammers, paint tins, paint brushes, screws, and screw drivers. On the shelf-less half wall, which meets the army green garage door, are golf clubs hanging from the wall in the same way one often sees snooker cues racked along a wall... Zaccariah has always considered golf to be the ruin of a perfectly good idea.

He begins to rummage around in a shoebox he finds on the floor under one of the shelves. It is full of photographs and newspaper cuttings. Lots of the photographs are of times and events of which he knows nothing. Sepia-people from a far off time; long forgotten faces meaningful to no one any longer. Personalities and characters – with thoughts, dreams, and problems that doubtlessly seemed fundamental at the time – which, like the clothes wrapped around their bodies and the shoes upon their feet, have long since disappeared into specks of dust.

And if it weren't for the photographs there'd probably be no trace that they ever existed. It was almost as if they had never been there at all. Maybe they *had* never existed at all, was the thought that burrowed its way into the centre of Zaccariah's mind. Maybe they are falsified photos, like the falsified life in which he now found himself.

As he delves deeper into the shoebox he notices that some of the newspaper clippings refer to him, or at least contain his name. But they are of a life he has never had. They have nothing to do with him, except that his name Zaccariah Chinnon appears in each of them.

There is one that has the headline 'Local boy Wins Scholarship To Gradlock', which had never happened. Some of the other articles Zaccariah finds even weirder. They are about periods, moments in his life, but with alterations. The stories are all nearly true, very nearly true, but with one or two details changed. Some of these cuttings he recognises from his own collection of bits and pieces, which he kept under his bed in his flat; and some are from the scrapbook his parents used to keep of him when he was a child.

One of the cuttings that he reads on that cold garage floor is about him scoring a hat-trick for his village football team. He remembers the match well, and a hat-trick had been scored for his team, but not by him… For several months he had been the regular striker for the team. In this particular match, he was substituted after half an hour for a new boy to the village. It was a Cup match, and the new boy had scored one just before half time, and the other two late in the second half. And that signalled the end of Zaccariah's automatic unchallenged selection for the team.

However, here, in this faded article from a faded time that never was – Zaccariah was the hero. It was solely due to Zaccariah's predatory goalmouth instincts that Cullham Utd Under 16s got through to the quarterfinals of the Cup. But it was all untrue…

Many of the articles in the box are along the same lines. Little insignificant episodes in his life had been taken and turned around. Without exception, the articles are about unhappy periods in his life; moments when the pattern of his life could have been markedly altered had X and Y occurred. But X and Y had not occurred, A and B had.

And Zaccariah had not been the *Hat-Trick Hero*; nor the *Star In the Making* in the school's production of Oliver Twist… And yet, according to these paragraphs on the floor in front of him, all that had gone before had turned out exactly the way that he'd hoped they would. Everything was 'corrected'. Everything had been rearranged so that it would fit into the vision of a perfectified world – and all for the benefit of Mr Kite… er… no no – all for the benefit of Mr Zaccariah Chinnon…

All the events, and tricky moments, that each person has to go through in the course of a normal life had been airbrushed out. They were all inconsequential things, none earth shattering and none life-destroying. They were all incidents that make one harder or more cynical. But now they were all gone: he'd dated the prettiest girls, got the top grades, been to the university he'd chosen as his first choice; and become a well thought of novelist.

------•••------

And such is life… Life is a labyrinthine, multifarious affair, with monsters and dark beings, and sometimes clowns with bells on their toes, taking turnings that confuse and complicate, and sometimes aid, one's path to the grave…

------•••------

Life was a dream – and dreams had become true.

VII

A light flickered and flashed. Cold. I feel cold. My senses are my friends, but I don't trust them here, now.

------•••------

I took the remnants of my coffee and stood in the passageway. I watched as green became grey, as suburbs became city. The intercom let us know that in a few minutes we would be arriving at our destination. I had been a long time away from the UK; I had been an even longer time away from London. The enormity and the impersonal nature of it all made me uneasy.

I had my rucksack with me and that was enough – more than enough. Sparks from the rails sizzled past the window. Metal against metal – we juddered to an inelegant halt. I heaved my rucksack down onto the platform, my rucksack that contained my useless belongings and my self-denials. A look-alike, a doppelganger, from a previous incarnation, from a time when I used to *be*, strode along the platform with beguiling purpose. If it was not her, and we had never met before, we would certainly not be meeting now. And anyway, my brain was tired.

But she was pretty, at least to my eyes, and deserved to be asked if she was who she could have been. She was too far ahead of me now though, and I did not dare. And what was the point in prolonging things…

The ticket man held out his hand… I found a station café, ordered a coffee, and chain-smoked till my time was up.

------•••------

"Darling?" Zaccariah hears coming from through the wall, and hurriedly shoves everything back into the shoebox. "What're you doing Zac?" enquires Ulla as her head appears in the doorway.

Zaccariah doesn't reply. Choosing instead to stare back at this woman in the black silk *faux* kung-fu dressing gown, and the rose coloured flip flops with an oversized plastic yellow daisy attached to the toe straps. He stares back with the edges of his mouth upturned. And in the Venn diagrams of life, this lip formation would fit into the circle marked 'smiles'. But whatever it was, it was defiant; maybe almost imperceptibly so – nevertheless *defiant* it was. And Zaccariah, quite apart from anything else, did not like to be called *Zac*. It was all too much 'Zig Zag Wanderer' for his liking.

"There's a decaff in the pot…" Ulla pauses after saying this, no doubt to give Zaccariah the space to respond, but Zaccariah just nods in silence. "I'll have a shower before I go," she continues… "Are you OK?"

"Fine," Zaccariah replies, this time with a more convincing smile. A smile which would more easily have fitted squarely into the 'Venn Smiles Circle'; unlike his earlier attempt which probably would have overlapped into another category entitled 'Facial Expressions' or 'Grimaces'.

"I'm running a bit late, you must have turned the alarm clock off by mistake," she utters in a mildly reprimanding manner. "It doesn't really matter, we just won't have time to breakfast together."

"Uh huh," Zaccariah grunts, washed with confusion and contempt for this absurd charade.

"We'll be away for a week, ten days at most… It'll do the children good to get away to the countryside and see their gran and granddad for a while."

Zaccariah shrugs and walks over to sit on a dusty paint-stained canvas camping chair.

"Look Zaccariah, I know you're a bit upset, but don't sulk darling." Again she pauses in anticipation of a response, but Zaccariah just gazes at some indeterminate point on the floor. "So I'll go and take my shower then... OK?"

"Fine."

"Right... see you in twenty then." And with that, Ulla about faces and leaves the kitchen.

Zaccariah 'knew' this was no dream. And he racked his brain to recall whether the last few articles he'd written had possibly gone too far, and this was his punishment. But he remembered nothing – nothing out of the ordinary. Nothing – except for the white box approaching out of the drizzle and the city gloom.

He felt he should run as fast as he could, for as long as he could, as far away as he could – until his heart was almost pounding out of his chest, and his lungs were rasping for air... But *why*, he asked himself. ...Why all this? It was like some enormous puzzle and he was in the middle of it. It was a mind game, and Zaccariah was a rat in a maze, a rabbit in a headlight – a man in a trap. But why... and where; that was the other thing – *where* was he? Yet, no – he would have to keep his wits about him. Punishing himself with all these questions would not help. If anything, he would just be playing into the hands of his enemy. He had to take a gradual approach, he told himself. See how the land lay. No sudden moves – no sudden decisions; take care and *think* before acting.

Zaccariah did not wish to put all his chickens into one coop just yet. One option was simply to lose it all together. Zaccariah smiled at this thought. The smile lasted a little longer than its natural life, for Zaccariah was also smiling at the fact that he had been able to make himself smile at all... Then fleetingly he dallied with this possibility as a serious option. What would become of him if he didn't play ball? What would they do (for the more he considered his predicament the more he hedged towards the idea of there being a *they*) if he went mad, or at least pretended to go mad? But, maybe that was what they wanted.

A passing thought was all it was though, and never really a serious option. Apart from anything else a vivid memory of an episode of the television serious Colditz shot through his mind. An episode which for some reason had struck him as a child.

During the Second Great War, if you were in an officers' prisoner of war camp and you ended up going insane you could get shipped off to your homeland. But whether this was a fact or just part of the storyline of the programme Zaccariah was not sure.

The television programme's twenty-eight episodes were based upon major Pat Reid's books about the endeavours of Allied officers to escape. Colditz Castle is in the town of the same name and is 48 km from the city of Leipzig.

When an officer or group of officers had an escape plan, it would have to be OK-ed by the escape committee. The particular episode that had momentarily popped into Zaccariah's mind was about a single officer's idea to simulate insanity. The officer in question put his idea to the escape committee: that he would be so convincing in his acting that it would not matter how closely he was scrutinised by the jailers, eventually they would have to accept that he had 'lost the plot', and send him home.

Despite the committee's initial misgivings, they eventually had to accept his assertion that his escape proposal was not one which would hinder any other simultaneous attempts to escape, and nor would it put anyone else in jeopardy.

Over time the officer became gradually more reclusive. Then he progressed to being, to say the least, eccentric. He and his fellow inmates ceased contact with each other, since they knew that he would be under constant surveillance. Eventually he began muttering to himself in the way that only lunatics (and occasionally geniuses) do. Walking around the recreational area giving rather more consideration to a stone he had picked up than was normal, a compatriot threw him a concerned glare – to which he returned the most minute of winks.

Said compatriot then went up to the inmates' common room where members of the escape committee had been having a rather concerned conversation about the present state of their friend. The officer who had been in the yard relayed his account of the scene involving their colleague's wink, which made them all a lot happier, and somewhat taken aback by his astounding acting abilities.

The unhinged behaviour of the officer continued unabated. Members of the escape committee and those in the know would occasionally give him a clandestine nod or a wink. Of course, they understood that it was too risky for him to make any gesture out of the 'abnormal' in response. His friends, now being more used to his behaviour and more confident that everything was going to plan, began to exchange tales of how well he was acting his part. Amongst themselves they would laugh about how convincingly he had behaved in a certain situation. They guffawed at how well, when approached by a camp guard, he had stared vacantly into the distance and began to dribble. Resulting in the guard shouting a few insults before stomping away. Eventually, whatever procedure had to be gone through was gone through – and he got sent back home to Blighty.

When his fellow internees heard of his release they had a secretive celebratory drink to his audacity.

Several weeks later, his former fellow captives received a letter. They knew who it was from because of the return address on the back of the envelope. Expectantly they opened the correspondence. It was, however, not from their former friend but from his spouse. She thanked everyone for being such good friends to her husband. And how she felt as though she knew all of them herself, because of how fondly her husband used to write about them in his letters before he got ill. She tells of how she visits him everyday since the mental institution where he now lives is not too far from their home…

"You did say you didn't want to come," Ulla continued.

As she spoke these words Zaccariah snapped out of his torpor, deciding that until he figured out what to do, the best thing was just to act as normally as he could. And by the sounds of it, his assigned wife would be going off somewhere shortly, and he would have the undisturbed run of the house.

"Yeah, no, that's fine. I was miles away..."

"Miles?"

"Yeah, still half asleep."

"Right? So you're OK about everything?"

"No really, you go ahead," he said... "Look, sorry about the alarm clock," he continued. "Maybe you've still got time for a quick coffee before you set off?"

"A decaff, certainly."

Zaccariah was rather pleased with how well he thought he had done. At least, he was pleased with how those on the outside of his head must have seen him. They would not have been expecting that. When she reports back to her superiors of his unmitigated acceptance of his new world, well, it would at least throw them, Zaccariah thought to himself.

"I'll be down in fifteen minutes... after I've soaped myself down," Ulla said, with what Zaccariah thought was a flirtatious raising of the eyebrows. "Anyway, why are you wearing those dirty old clothes?" But before Zaccariah had come up with a feasible response to this legitimate question, Ulla added, "come up and get changed." What accompanied these last words bizarrely looked almost like pleading eyes.

She held out her hand. His gaze darted from her walnut brown eyes to her outstretched hand and back again. And this supplication launched him hesitantly out of his preoccupations. He noted how her hand had no grip to it. And so he wrapped his palm around her fingers and thought that *maybe* she was a friendly ghost after all...

On arriving in the bedroom she sat on the edge of the bed in preparation for unbuttoning. Zaccariah stood in the doorway.

"Turn the shower on for me, will you darling?"

He looked at her, not really knowing what he was doing. Then again, it did not really matter – the garage or the bedroom, it was all the same. He must remain vigilant; act normally, yet remain vigilant. She gave him a friendly wink. By the time he had reached the bathroom and been flooded by the glare of the strip lighting, Ulla had taken off her Kung-Fu style silk dressing gown.

Ulla made her way over to the bathroom and closed the door behind her. Zaccariah was leaning into the shower attempting to put the shower on without getting his arm wet. His arm did get wet – icy cold wet. There was a time delay between pushing the shower button in and the water cascading out. Not much of a delay, but enough to lead the uninitiated into thinking that 'contact' had not been made. It was on the reintroduction of his arm into the shower unit to give the shiny metal button another push that the water came flooding out, and soaked his arm.

As he turned away from the shower he heard the click of the bathroom door closing. And there in front of him was an early thirty-something woman with messed-up dark hair in black bra and knickers, who one and a half hours ago he had never seen before in his life. They looked at each other. She smiled an asexual smile, and as she reached behind with her two arms to unclip her bra she said, "I'd like you to get in with me." She looked down, shyly averting her gaze, as she uttered these words. This, thought Zaccariah, certainly was not the manner in which a lover, even a pretend lover, made such a proposal.

Before Zaccariah could think of a response, Ulla held him with her gaze once again, and said "Please." And seeing the doubt on Zaccariah's face, she punctuated her plea with a reassuring nod. Hypnotised by incomprehension his left hand unconsciously dropped to the top button of his trousers and flicked it undone. Ulla put her bra on the side next to the washbasin. Zaccariah turned from facing her – for which she gave him a little rub on his back, as if to thank him for his discretion.

From the reflection in the mirror, he could see Ulla looking in one of the drawers that was under the sink unit. Her breasts were small. Triangles that emerged from her chest like miniature Aztec pyramids. The shadows of a former day on the beach, maybe with her real husband, made her bust paler than the rest of her body. She slid the top drawer shut and began rummaging through the one below. Not finding whatever it was she was searching for she turned, plucked the sumptuous towel off its rail and sidled round the back of Zaccariah. He was conscious of her buttocks sliding against his as she passed. She reached round the corner of the cubicle and hung her towel on the metal peg. She temperature-checked the water with her hand, peeled her knickers off, shook them from around her ankles, and stepped in. Zaccariah watched as she positioned herself under the stream of water and tilted her head back. With her eyes closed she rubbed her hands over her face, forehead, and through her hair.

The bathroom reminded Zaccariah of a motel bathroom, all pristine and appearing unused. He could not be sure it had not been used before. But it looked so sparkling and shiny-new he almost expected to see miniature tablets of soap still in their wrappings, and those tomato ketchup style sachets of shampoo with only enough sweet smelling liquid in them for one head of hair...

Zaccariah thought that maybe this supposed partner of his had snuck into bed only a couple of hours before the alarm had gone off. Or possibly she had been given her assignment weeks ago, and had been living in the house for some time already – to get used to her new surroundings prior to his 'abduction'. Being as well acquainted with the layout of the house as possibly could help her in her role. But then why was she going away so soon? And where were these children she had mentioned?

Ulla dropped her shoulder slightly and turned her head. "Come on in," she said. Zaccariah took his T-shirt off and stepped in behind her. As she was turning to face him he noticed that she had a small tattoo on the top of her left arm. But he only got the briefest of glimpses, and wasn't able to make out what it was. "Right," she said decisively as the warm water trickled over and between them, "I haven't got very long, so listen."

"What...?"

"Just listen, please... You... *We*," she quickly corrected herself, "are being watched... There are only three places in the house where you can't be heard, and only two of those where you can't be seen either."

"What *are* you talking about?" Zaccariah's brain was like a rowing boat getting pounded against the rocks of some unknown shoreline.

"Look, please listen. I'm risking a lot doing this."

"Where the fuck am I? How do I get back home? And..."

"Look," Ulla interrupted, "we really don't have time... and I don't know the answers to all your questions. So why not stop wasting time and listen to what I *can* tell you."

"Who are you anyway?" Zaccariah continued, ignoring what she had just said.

"I can get out of this shower right now, and walk out the door and…"

"OK, OK, but how do I know I can trust you?"

"You don't," replied Ulla. "But I don't think you have a choice, do you?" Zaccariah nodded in acknowledgement of the predicament he was in. "So," she went on, "in here with the water running we can't be seen or heard; the shed at the bottom of the garden is also reasonably safe; and in the corner of the garage where you were sitting you can be seen but not heard, if you speak quietly."

"Why are you helping me?" asked Zaccariah, still not sure if he really was being helped.

"Because it serves my purposes to do so. Be under no illusions Zac…"

"Zaccariah!"

"Be under no illusions *Zac*, I'm helping you because by doing so it edges me a little closer to my ultimate objectives."

"Which are?"

"Nothing that would mean anything to you… and I have neither the time nor the inclination to go into it all with you now. Sufficed to say that there's an 'us' and a 'them' – there always is," she snorted disparagingly. "Cowboys and Indians. And I'm one of the goodies but, yes I know, I would say that wouldn't I… I'm one of the Indians, the good guys – but we're up against it… You've been put here by the 'them'. And the 'them' think I'm one of them, but I'm not. And, since you've been taken and put where you are it sort of makes you a *de facto* one of 'us'. But, don't get it too much into your head that what I'm doing is for you, it's not – it's more *against* them."

"How can you be sure that I won't walk out of this bathroom and announce to whoever's watching exactly what you've just told me?"

"Because firstly, and most importantly, it wouldn't do you any good. It wouldn't help you in your situation; it would just make trouble for me. Big trouble. And someone who would play everything by the book might well replace me... There wouldn't be one stray ray of sunlight filtering in the reality of the situation to you... and under those circumstances even the sanest of minds must go a little crazy. And secondly, when you finally have time to reflect on everything that has happened to you in such a short space of time, when I go away and leave you for two weeks..."

"I thought you said a week or ten days, before," interrupted Zaccariah whilst straining to see Ulla's tattoo.

"Yeah, that's how long I'm supposed to tell you. But I don't return until you've been on your own for a little over two weeks... And during my time away, you'll think about what I've told you here over and over again. And you'll sway from trusting me to distrusting me, and back again. And in your moments of distrusting me – you'll play with the idea that this was all part of 'it': that this whole conversation and your reaction to it was all some kind of test. And then in your especially paranoid moments, you'll query if my telling you *this* was also some kind of clever double bluff. And for a while you'll go round in circles. Circles that there are no way of breaking... You see, you don't know enough to be able, with any real confidence, to fall on one side or the other. And, by the way, the other reason why I don't think you'll 'announce' what I've been telling you is because of this circle you'll spend so much of your time navigating. In the end it'll just be faith – belief. In the end you'll just have to believe me or not. And I figure that you'll come to the conclusion that you may as well give me the benefit of the doubt... because, well, what choice do you really have? So, I don't think you'll give me away – 'cos I'm the best bet you've got honey."

Without hesitation or change of tone she asked Zaccariah if he would like to make love on the bed. He shook his head, and felt like a naughty school child who'd been sent to stand in the corner of the class: startled and unsure.

Ulla laughed. "Don't you find me attractive?" Zaccariah shrugged. "Take your chances Zac... grab 'em while they're there." And she giggled... but on seeing his eyes and realising she was being a little cruel, she rubbed him tenderly on his arm. Zaccariah gave her a weak smile in response, and then turned to exit the cubicle. "Wait," she said whilst lightly holding his shoulder. He only half turned back, making it perfectly clear that he had had enough.

"Just a couple of other things: in *this* place you're a journalist and you work from home; your office is at the end of the landing, opposite the stairs. In a week or so, a woman who is supposedly a friend of mine will come to the door looking for me. She'll invite herself in – don't trust her! And when I return I'd like us to have another shower together. You can tell me how you're getting on, and I can tell you if I've found anything else out."

Zaccariah began to lift his leg to step out of the shower, but Ulla applied a little more pressure to his shoulder.

"Don't forget, as soon as you leave this room we don't mention another word of any of this. And you have to act towards me the same way as before."

Zaccariah flicked his shoulder forward and he was standing dripping on the carpet. He grabbed the towel marked 'Zac'. He quickly rubbed his legs and feet to prevent the rug getting any wetter. He worked his way up. Roughly towelling his feather-cut greying brown ear-length hair, and whilst momentarily resting his face in the towel he noticed the label sewn into the border seam. It had some writing on it – washing instructions, and a small round symbol like the one that had been on the breast pocket of the pyjamas he had been in when he had first awoken. Some department store logo, he figured. But it not being one he was aquatinted with meant... well, what did it mean? ...It meant that maybe he was in a different land. Then, less drastically, he concluded that he could possibly simply be in another part of the same land. He could be in a region of the country he wasn't familiar with, one that might have different merchandising outlets.

He turned to ask Ulla where he could find some deodorant. She had her back to him and was shampooing her hair. He looked at her slender form and wondered if at another time in another place sex could have been on the cards. There was no question that

Ulla — not that for a moment he believed that to be her real name — was pretty, very pretty. Which he guessed was probably one of the main reasons why she had been chosen for this part.

But he did not trust her. There was no way that 'they', whoever they were, would have given her such a role without thoroughly checking her out first... If they could do everything that they'd done to him, they certainly would have made sure that she was unquestionably *with* them. And he just could not imagine sleeping with someone so calculating and two-faced. But she was very pretty, he noted again as his eyes followed a soap sud sliding from her head down the nape of her neck and down half of her back before getting disintegrated by a splash of water.

"Where's the deodorant?" he repeated a little louder since she hadn't heard him the first time.

"Have you tried in the drawers?" And as she turned to give him what he considered to be a rather vague reply, he was finally able to make out the design of the tattoo on her shoulder. It was another one of those cryptic circles, shaded on one side and with four parallel lines of differing lengths on the other.

This was taking brand loyalty too far, he thought. More than just worrying, he found it to be sinister. What kind of identifying mark was this? Bizarrely, he thought, Ulla and the towel and pyjamas must all come from the same place, they must all come from the same... from the same... or, they must all have some kind of affinity with something or other. With... with, some view or outlook or approach to... to, something or other. They were all integrally connected to some design for life, some view of how to approach life, of how to live one's life. Was it a barcode of sorts, and Ulla was a product, a product that had been brainwashed into trying to brainwash him?

For all he knew he could be right in the middle of a totalitarian state. As far as Zaccariah could tell, in his new little world, the invasion of his private life was total. He did not know what was going on outside, or up the street, or round the corner — all he knew was that the truth was at the bottom of an in-tray piled high with sheets upon sheets of rubberstamped bullshit.

He exited the bathroom with his towel tucked around his waist, and went and sat on the bed. Putting his elbows on his knees, he rested his face in his hands. He pressed the palms of his hands tightly against his face so that even with his eyes open he could only see black. He closed his eyelids and pressed hard against his eyeballs until little white flecks appeared inside his head. The calming affect that this created led him to push a little harder – until he could make out the occasional pattern floating around in the emptiness. His eyeballs began to send messages of pain to his brain. He wanted to scratch away the surface and burrow inside his head, roll up into a ball and be forgotten…

Downstairs, dressed in light cotton cream-coloured trousers and white un-tucked grandfather shirt and blue and white-striped espadrilles – all of which fitted him perfectly – he put the coffee on, and got acquainted with the layout of the kitchen. He flicked the egg-shaped matt black radio on, hoping for a sweet sounding song and maybe a little information to go on.

"**We are all lines within the circle**" – came the voice from the radio, followed by some white noise and then a short burst of high-pitched beeps and dashes. Then came a second voice:

"…Ladies and gentlemen of the jury – this man is innocent. This I know. So, the reason we are all here today is not in fact as might first appear; namely, to ascertain whether or not this man is innocent or guilty. He is innocent – that is a fact. It is rather, ladies and gentlemen, learned colleagues, *I* who am on trial. For it is my job, with clever turns of phrase and jovial asides, to persuade, cajole, and convince you of this man's unequivocal innocence. And if I fail, members of the jury, and you do ultimately find this man guilty of the crimes for which he has been brought before you today – please bear in mind that this does not in fact mean that this man is guilty. He is not. It merely means that in your eyes the prosecuting counsellor has been more convincing than I have. The man is innocent – irrespective of whether he is found to be so or not. Justice will either be done or it won't be done; either way he is still innocent.

Finally, ladies and gentlemen of the jury, and I also address our colleagues in the gallery who the lottery has chosen to be our 'button pushers' for today's event, I would ask you to carefully consider these last two points: firstly, please reflect upon the meaning of '...beyond reasonable doubt'. If you are not as sure as this expression requires, then you must find this man not guilty. For, and this leads me to my second point, is it not more desirable for a guilty man to go free than for an innocent man to..."

The radio looked as though it had been spray-painted. Zaccariah pressed a couple of switches, fiddled with an unmarked dial, and put the coffee on. Zaccariah did not wish to listen to plays or stories. He did not want to listen to words; he had had enough of his own words floating around. He wanted instruments, music, a band, preferably without a vocalist.

Eventually he came across some wallpaper-sound: fast-food instant gratification plastic music. Normally he would not have given this pop pap the time of day – but right now, this sterilised toilet-fresh music that did not even require a minimal degree of intellectual or spiritual effort on his part was exactly what he required: sound just above the status of silence. Enough to soften his spiralling thoughts, without drowning them out completely... Nietzsche, he reflected, said that "Without music life would be a mistake."

The coffee spluttered and spat, and beckoned Zaccariah over. He took the pot off the stove and set it down on the olive green table. The table at full stretch would have made a circle. In its present state it was an oblong – with its two flaps folded away hanging down against its central column. It would have been possible to have half of it unfolded, but the table's full circle would have left barely enough room to pass. It was situated against the wall under the clock that read thirty-three zero one.

He sat on a stool and poured himself a fresh, if rather tasteless, coffee. He decided to have another look at the newspaper until Ulla descended. This time he noticed the circle and the three lines in the top right hand corner of the title page. Very small, just underneath some serial number or other. The front page had a picture of some wizened old crow wearing a crumpled hat and holding something aloft that could just have easily been a stick or a cucumber. She was smiling into the lens in front of what was presumably her residence. All this took place under the headline: 'Don't Forget To Let the Cat Out!'. Zaccariah could not muster up enough curiosity to read beyond those first seven words.

His coffee mug was white with black upside-down hearts all over it. It was designed so that the spaces in between the black hearts made white hearts. In this sense, depending upon how you looked at it, it could also have been a black mug with white hearts on it. It was like the Escher picture of the candlestick and the two faces, thought Zaccariah. He lifted his mug up, and sure enough on the underneath was the circle with the four lines. It was gradually becoming more a case of what didn't have this design on it than what did. And it was more than just a trademark, it was identification; it was more than a brand – it was branding…

"We would like to welcome all new comers to zone five. Things may seem strange, but you are welcome, you are guests, and maybe for the first time in your lives you are free… we are all lines within the circle," came the monotone delivery in between indistinguishable tracks.

Zaccariah heard Ulla nimbly clicking down the stairs. She appeared at the doorway in a smoky grey jumpsuit zipped open to her cleavage, what little she had. Her plastic orange boots and an orange handkerchief tucked into the breast pocket were the only splashes of colour. It was strange attire, especially considering the weather outside – a cross between a ski outfit and a pilot's uniform. She waited in the entrance of the kitchen until Zaccariah looked up, and gave him what she considered to be a reassuring wink. She sat down on the other stool and poured herself a decaff, and then went over to the fridge to get some milk.

The next fifteen minutes she spent telling Zaccariah about the street, about the neighbours and their foibles. She very cleverly pitched her conversation at just the right level. Making it sound like any normal kitchen sink conversation and yet being as informative as possible. Using phrases such as 'You remember when Mr Mandin...' and, 'you know how much she dislikes...' So that no eavesdropper would have realised that Zaccariah was hearing all about these people for the first time. And Zaccariah listened and smiled in all the right places, knowing that soon she would be gone.

"What are you reading that rag for?" she asked while tapping her finger on the paper in front of him. "Have you seen your latest piece yet?" She got up, went into the living room, and returned with a more professional looking newspaper in her hands. She fingered through it for several moments while she remained standing.

"Ah, there it is," she said, and laid the opened newspaper down on the table.

Zaccariah saw his name at the top of a full-page article. Well, the shortened more zippy version of his name, which belonged to nothing more than a motel-fluffy towel in the bathroom of this show home.

Lifting his head up from the newspaper, Zaccariah asked: "Is Mr Mandin really as bad as all that?"

"Oh yes, I was talking to him in front of his driveway last week and you know what he did? He put his hand on my bottom. Quite matter-of-factly, in the middle of a sentence, he gave my behind a couple of pats, if you please. I mean the cheek of that man is unbelievable."

"What did you do?"

"Well, what could I do? I made my excuses and left pretty sharpish. But I tell you if he does it again I'll have to say something… His wife was in the front garden; it's her I feel sorry for. But I don't care if his wife's there or not, if he does anything like that again I'll give him a piece of my mind. I will… You know Mrs O'Neill on the corner – well, she thinks he's having an affair with somebody at his work, she told me the name but I've forgotten it… anyway, I find that very hard to believe. I think he's simply, well, you know, just the way he is… slimy, you know. But I bet you if any woman called his bluff and came on back to him, he'd run a mile. I bet you. Really, I mean, what woman in her right mind would want anything to do with that Brylcreem beanpole?" The end of Ulla's outburst was punctuated with a little nervous laugh.

She was a great actress, thought Zaccariah… He began to read the article and was vaguely aware of Ulla brushing past him. He heard a slight rattling at the other end of the kitchen, but didn't pay any attention. She came back and sat opposite him, putting a plate of pastries on the table. Absent-mindedly Zaccariah reached over for one and, without taking his eyes from the article, took a bite from it.

"I've filled the freezer up, so you won't have to bother doing any shopping while I'm away," said Ulla.

Zaccariah read on. It was indeed an article that he had written. But as with the 'memorabilia' from his life that he had found in the garage, changes had been made… It was a piece that he had written a few months earlier, a little before the white box had begun appearing.

It was something he had written during one of his less circumspect periods. It was written words from a time when his increasing frustration with the régime was beginning to result in carelessness. What he was now reading however, was a straight down the line rather dry piece of prose.

It was the kind of thing he might have written in his younger days, when he had been oblivious to what was really going on. It was humourless, unchallenging stuff… It was writing that had been changed from what he had written into some surgically clean articulation of the world seen through the eyes of the authorities. There were no longer any of his jaunty asides, or satirical digressions. And certainly all the coded criticism of those in power had disappeared. All that was left of his original piece were the bare facts.

"So that's why I'm here," said Zaccariah as he raised his eyes from the newspaper.

"Sorry?"

"So that's why I'm here," he repeated angrily, whilst holding the paper up with his left hand and stabbing it with his right. The centre pages of the newspaper fell firstly onto his knees and then slowly slid down his legs onto the floor. "Because of my articles," he continued. "They didn't like the fact that I wasn't an unwavering card-carrying member of the 'everything's alright here really' club... *And* I let my readers know it."

Ulla made an egregious turn of her head to look up at the clock on the wall (which appeared to have stopped ticking) – when a mere raising of the eyeballs would not only have been sufficient, but common practice – and exclaimed: "Oh my sweet master's keeper, is that the time? I'll be late for the children." This she said whilst conspicuously avoiding eye contact with Zaccariah.

He thought to himself, that this was the first time he had seen her even slightly flustered. Certainly, it was the first time that she had given anything but an award-winning performance...

She leaned over the table and kissed Zaccariah on the cheek. She squeezed his hand, which was resting on the table, and said: "Look after yourself Zac. Stay and finish your breakfast... I'll see myself out." And with a wink and a blown kiss she turned and scuttled off. He picked up another pastry and made his way through to the living room to watch her departure.

As he reached the living room he just caught a glimpse of the outside world through the doorway. Then, as Ulla hastily slammed the door shut behind her, it was gone... And it was not the world of sunny suburban comfortable mediocrity. It was grey, smoky, and damp, with some enormous towering concrete edifice only feet away from the front door. He also caught a split second of someone else in a jumpsuit, but with a mole-snout gas mask on, waving from by the corner of the edifice that matched the colour of the sky.

Zaccariah's tortured mind reached for some reference point, but there was none. And his eyes darted from the now shut chrome plated door to the windows that nearly reached up to the level of the ceiling... But somehow, through the windows another reality was being portrayed: one of squeaky-clean suburban sobriety, and the fascination with the inconsequential.

Through the window a red sports car had just pulled up across the road; a sprinkler was revolving on the Thomas' front lawn. Mrs Mandin's gloved hand could be seen tugging at something herbaceously unsavoury. The sun shone and all was well with the world. And like being threatened by a twisted Scandinavian mask-wearer, he knew he had to get out before this abnormal world acquired a certain normality to it. He had to get out before the dark skies and the gasmasks he was sure he'd seen through the door either drove him insane, or he began doubting what he'd seen.

The cold white-light white box is the last thing he remembered prior to falling asleep and waking up in this strange land. Consequently, he knew he could not be sure of anything. Not her, not what she was telling him, not even of himself and his own feelings. And he needed to get out of there as quickly as he could.

What was happening to his mind? What was going on in the skies? And he needed to know which route signposted the return to sanity? A pristine windowpane and the chug-chug lifestyle of the commuter belt? Or, a bleeding sky and a myopic fug-snout grey mask, and a fear-ridden metallic-clink prayer-mat embrace to the future?

"You Bitch!" he cried out from the primal depths of his guts. He ran and pulled at the door handle, but it was locked. He then retreated a few steps and charged the door, taking a leap so as to kick the door with the full force of his outstretched foot. The door rattled slightly, but nothing more. He seized the handle – yanking it down and up. He shoulder barged the door. He kicked and kicked at it until the sole of his foot could take no more… He ran over to the television, the rage throbbing through his veins, and lifted it off its stand. He raised it above his head and launched it at the window. It fell to the ground, bounced slightly, and rolled onto its screen. There was not so much as a scratch to the window, and the television was intact apart from one of the black knobs from the back that had snapped off.

Zaccariah snatched the flower vase from on the floor next to the bookshelf and hurled it at the window. Nothing. It bounced off and flew to the ground. Panting and puffy eyed he bent and grabbed what looked like a brick from the hearth. It turned out, however, to be a fake: made out of a very hard rubbery material.

Then, not quite knowing what to do next, his eyes searched the room for familiarity, or a story, or inspiration. Then, as his gaze once again settled on the front door a thought hit him. And he turned and ran into the kitchen to the back door. He snapped down the handle – locked. He seemed to recollect, but only vaguely, that there had been a key in the lock when he had first come down. Then he recalled that when he had been reading his article in the newspaper, Ulla had slipped past him and he had heard a nondescript metallic rattle, which must have been Ulla taking the key out.

The garden through the backdoor looked the way it had looked twenty minutes ago… and an hour ago. It was not a garden at all though, was it? It was a concrete land. The garden, the house, everything, was a mirage, a false paradise. Even if he did manage to escape from this shag-pile prison, what then? What would he be escaping into? A place where the sun did not shine, and people wore oxygen masks?

From the brief glimpse he'd stolen of the outside world, it appeared as if the house was maybe on some kind of industrial estate. Possibly his was not the only house, and he was not the only dog waiting for some non-existent buzzer. Maybe there were others like him, maybe just next door, maybe where the garden was supposed to be…

Zaccariah's thoughts were like plumes of noxious smoke circling up into the sulphur-streaked skies. His eyes swept around the kitchen for something to pick the lock with. He riffled through drawers. He snatched open cupboards so they clattered one after another against their frames, but was unable to find anything suitable.

He dashed upstairs with the intention of finding a metal coat hanger. On reaching the top of the stairs however, his attention was drawn to the partially open door that purported to be his study. He stuck his head through the gap. But there was nothing of interest that stood out: a desk with a few scattered pens and pieces of paper on it.

Zaccariah was out of breath, and after taking several moments to compose himself he entered the office and went over to the window. First he tried the latch, but of course it wouldn't budge; then he noted that the view through the window was of the side of the Mandins' house. And if he put his head right next to the windowpane, he could see a slither of their front garden as well. A slither which at that moment had Mrs Mandin lopping off the head of something while kneeling down with a yellow plastic bucket by her feet... Ah, Mrs Mandin – the gardener *extraordinaire*. What *did* she do with herself in the cold weather, what did she do with herself in *real* life?

Then suddenly a realisation snapped at him like a crocodile in a swamp, and Zaccariah turned and ran down the landing and launched himself down the stairs. Missing out two and three steps at a time he reached the bottom and dashed to the living room window. Stopping himself with his two hands, he put his head against the cold pane and could see the gloved weeding hand of Mrs Mandin through the bush that separated both houses. He hurtled back upstairs, back to the study, only to see Mrs Mandin standing up attacking some poor unsuspecting plants with what looked like pruning shears. Panting, he did it all over again, slightly slower this time, and sure enough out of the downstairs window Mrs Mandin was still on all fours. Zaccariah flopped back onto the sofa and laughed a laugh that rapidly transformed into the tears of a desperate man.

The silver domed-shape space-age-looking carriage clock that had been on the television and now lay on the floor read thirty-three hours and one minute. Zaccariah saw it with a vacant stare, but, too tired and numb to think, it did not register. Exhausted, he pushed himself up and dejectedly climbed the stairs. And, sapped of energy he undressed and pulled the covers over his head.

The sleep was long and deep, and filled with strange narcotic-like dreams. Bright colours, connections, sparkling electricity, and an on-off switch, and a sense of a deeper understanding... They were the kinds of dreams that are life-like and make some crazy warped sense the moment you awake. Then hours, even minutes, later, great chunks have disappeared; and all that remains are vague random images and short sequences. And any initial sense or logic becomes nothing more than a distant fuzzy memory. Or there is no memory at all.

Zaccariah awoke with a motel-room lack of recognition. Then after several seconds staring at an unblemished ceiling, recollection stole into his psyche. And with it, desolation once again swept over him. His heavy head felt as though it were moving through thick translucent soup as he idly noticed one of the bedroom windows was open. The curtain rippled in the soft afternoon breeze. Then almost like a cartoon double take, a thought juddered into Zacarriah's scrambled mind.

He whipped back the bedclothes and darted over to the other side of the bed. Naked he stood and peered at the scene out of the window. He tentatively reached his hand out of the open window. Incomprehensibly to Zaccariah it was not all merely an optical illusion – and his hand did not come up against some invisible barrier. Satisfied he wasn't about to be fried, he thrust his head out and felt the gentle soothing breeze on his face.

The view was the same, the same as he had seen through the closed window. The sun was lower, silhouetting the trees; the breeze looked brisker and the clouds were corrugating across the sky. Essentially though, it was the same view he had seen out of every glass panel since he had arrived. There was no trace of the concrete world he'd glimpsed through the front door.

He grabbed a book called The Cubist's House from the dressing table and wedged it in between the window and the frame. The outside world was accessible, and he was damn sure it was going to remain so. He decided he'd get dressed and get out of there as quickly as he could. He'd climb out of the window and down the drainpipe. He didn't want to risk going downstairs and checking if he could open the front door. How hellish it would be, he thought, if the front door turned out to be closed, and when he galloped back upstairs the window was shut fast as well. No – the chance to flee had presented itself and he was going to make sure he took it.

Two middle-aged men were conferring with each other outside number thirty-seven. The one with the triangular face and the Toulouse Lautrec beard was wearing a slightly tilted-back bowler hat with what looked like a spike coming out of the top of it. The spike looked like an arrowhead, or more like the head of a wrought-iron railing. The man momentarily disengaged his attention from what his companion was saying and, on seeing Zaccariah watching them both, gave a wave. More accurately would be to describe it as a salute rather than a wave, however. Of course, a wave is a form of salutation – but this greeting, or acknowledgement, had a more formal quality to it: it started with a vertically held hand pressed against the ridge of the nose and forehead, while the thumb pointed towards the ear at a 45° angle. The 'V' shape that this created framed the eye. Then, in one single movement, the hand was moved to the side of the head where it made circular regal-like motions. Zaccariah nodded in return.

The angle at which he had wedged open the window meant that as Zaccariah turned away from it he could see a reflection in the dressing table mirror. The image was of his back reflected from the opened window. It was by no means a diamond clear image, mingled as it was with the light and the clouds and the sky from outside. Nevertheless, it was clear enough. Clear enough for him to make something out that he had not previously seen... On his back was a tattoo, a picture, a symbol. It consisted of a circle, half of which was black, the other half of which was white with four vertical lines of varying lengths in it. Written around the outside of this circle were the words: *We are all lines within the circle.*

"And that's where I've got to," announced Slinky in a self-satisfied tone. "Good, huh?"

"Yeah, great. But I want to know what happens next?"

"Yes, but I don't know what happens next, do I?"

"No, no, I know. But... well... I've got to buy a copy... Who's the author?

"Bruno Schleinstein," said Slinky.

"Don't be funny!"

"What? Bruno Schleinstein's the author."

"No, he can't be."

"Why not?"

"Well, that's the name of the actor who was in several of Werner Herzog's films."

"Oh."

"Yeah… you know, he played Kaspar Hauser, for example. So, well, he can't be the author."

"Oh – I don't know about all that… I don't go to the cinema much."

"What? You don't know who Bruno… or, I mean, you don't even know who Werner Herzog is?"

"Um… maybe the name I… er… might have heard before. But look, the author *is* Bruno Schleinstein. It says it there on the spine." And she held the book up in front of me.

"Um, bizarre…" I said as I redirected my gaze from her book to the road again. "Must be a different Bruno Schleinstein," I added thoughtfully. But I did find it odd… *do* find it odd. Especially since after the films of the *Nouvelle Vague*, Herzog was one of my favourite directors…

Then I fell silent, and so did she. And my thoughts floated out of the window and up to the blue sky.

We drove, or I have the feeling we drove, a while longer. The scenery had long since disappeared. At least to my mind it had, although I had not noticed it at the time. Or, if I had, it had not really registered… Slinky had gone. Maybe I had dropped her off somewhere near Salamanca. I do not remember. The road faded gradually. First, the white lines became less defined, and soon they were indistinguishable from the rest of the road. Then the road, the sky and the surroundings merged into a fuzzy grey noiselessness. The light flickered several times – as if it were lightning from a silent electric sky. And I was left sitting in a dissolving car.

The last thing I remember was still sitting in the driver's seat holding tightly onto the steering wheel. All else was gone. Everything had disappeared – except for me.

VIII

My dreams are like thoughts. And my thoughts are like memories. And if I had ever got to write that book or even make a film, it would have been a little like this... And it feels like there are poachers in my house, and every mirror bears my name.

------•••------

After Portugal I returned to Britain. And then... then... that's it, I went to Berlin.

Berlin is a city of cranes, trains, and men at work. A city sprinting headlong towards the future with its feet firmly planted in the past. It remains an island in a sea of history. A crossroads between past and present; old ideas and new trends; East and West; DDR and BRD... The new German capital is a city of flux – blink and you might miss something. A place deliciously ebbing and flowing with the tides of change.

Construction is everywhere, lapping at your heels around every corner. As you walk past the Brandenburg Gate to Potsdammer Platz, you are unable to avoid the rather surreal sight of what must be the largest building site in Europe, with great metal monsters penetrating the skyline from every conceivable angle.

And I remember that I never ceased to be pleasantly surprised by the cultural nooks and crannies I kept coming across. I lived in Mitte, which was the centre of the old Eastern part of the city...

A stone's throw from my coal-heated flat that dated from between the wars was a little cinema run by an elderly Czech couple. After paying for your ticket at the door, you passed a little hole in the wall where you could purchase bottles of beer or glasses of wine from the elderly woman. Then with your free hand, you had to push the partitioning curtain to one side to reveal the twenty-three-seat cinema.

In front of each of the four rows of seats were a couple of small round tables for you to put your drinks on, with ashtrays for you to flick your ash into whilst watching the story unfold. On each of the three separate occasions that I visited this cinema the old gentleman made his way to the front to announce what the film was, which country it originated from, and who the director was, before going to the projection room to run the film. Afterwards, if it was the last showing of the day, most people would stay on for a few drinks and a chat with the elderly couple. Apart from myself, most people appeared to know each other, and although I was made to feel most welcome, it was a regulars' cinema. A cinema to which people had most likely been going for years – quite probably since well before these days of Unification.

Unannounced and unassuming, this little musty smelling movie theatre, which you could quite easily pass without noticing if you did not know it was there, was, for me, a throwback to a more clandestine time when certain activities probably had to be kept as cloistered as possible.

Following my last visit to this cinema I finished off my evening at a literally underground club, in which you had to stoop because of the low and crumbling ceiling. Drinks were served from behind the makeshift bar in plastic cups, and the music came from someone's portable stereo. When I asked where the toilets were, I was told that they were on the fifth floor of the building. On entering the loos of this antiquated squatted building, I spotted a mug in front of the mirror with five toothbrushes in it... The following week when I tried to return, the club had gone, not a trace of it remained. That is the way it was all the time, and that was part of the excitement of living in Berlin: there was always something new to discover, and nothing stood still.

One day I went for a stroll to investigate the area around where I lived. It was one of those winter days that seemed so prevalent during my short time in the new German capital. A perfectly round orange burning disc was perched on the horizon, which took the edge off the chill of the crisp nose-numbing air.

I wrapped up warm in a long Russian army overcoat I had bought from an outdoor market the week before. And I felt that I looked the part for stalking around the streets of the former spy capital of the world: I was equipped for the harshest of Siberian winds, and ready for any poisoned umbrella that might come my way. And so I set off for a day of constructively aimless wandering around.

I headed for what remained of the Wall. Since the beginning of its construction on the 12th August 1961, artists were drawn to this modern age monolith. Passers-by, art students, and internationally respected artists had all, in their time, adorned the Wall with their outpourings on what was the largest canvas in history.

I kept going with no particular destination in mind, to get acquainted with this city I had decided to make my new home; and to absorb the atmosphere and get a sense of the history seeping out of the cracks in the buildings. I eventually found myself at the Bauhaus Museum. 'Bauhaus' was a school of art and design that wanted to unify all the creative arts under the primacy of architecture. Due to its liberal, left wing, and modernist tendencies the Nazis dissolved it in 1933. The thing that strikes one about the Bauhaus furniture, for example, is how un-striking it is; how normal and everyday it appears. Clearly a testament to how ahead of its time it was.

After stopping for a sandwich, a coffee, and a chat at a Turkish roadside eatery, I decided it was time to head for home and set about the performance of lighting the coal oven. An intricate procedure that involved the pulling of knobs, and sliding along of metal plates to ensure that just enough but not too much air was getting to the firelighters and scrunched up pieces of newspaper.

I was tired, the sun was setting, and I had strayed far enough away from my flat to merit getting the tram back. I stood at the tram-stop watching the fellow smokers trying to determine at which point their exhalation ceased being cigarette smoke and started to become breath again. A slow prolonged screech and a clunk heralded the arrival of the tram. I boarded, greeted the driver, and clicked my ticket. Out of my window I could see the slowly sinking sun reflecting off the shiny radio tower that dominates the skyline of the old Russian Sector of the city.

My nearest tram stop was about half a mile from my front door. I alighted and made my way along the pavement. Collar up and head down, scarf tightened and hands in pockets; and I looked like a spy on a mission. Or, I looked the way I imagined a spy on a mission would look… As I scurried along, I hoped that by some chance there might at least be a few glowing embers left in my fire, so that I would not have to go through the whole rigmarole of lighting the only means of warmth I had in my flat from scratch. I did not hold out much hope though.

As these thoughts, along with the breeze, swirled around my head, my gaze was suddenly drawn to the bizarre sight of a dog poo with a little American flag in it. Now it is not often these days that we have cause to laugh out loud in public, maybe a little titter on a train whilst reading an amusing book, but that is about it. This, however, was one of those rare occasions that deserved the outburst of an uncontrollable roar of laughter…

When I eventually regained my composure, I continued on my way. A few yards up the pavement, still smiling away to myself, I looked down and spotted another canine poo, of a slightly lighter hue, with another toothpick sized American flag planted in its curly summit.

And as I progressed, now with my eyes fixed firmly on the ground, I happened upon another doggie doo with yet another American flag piercing its handsome crown, and then another and another and another, all the way up the pavement. Maybe ten in total, topped off with the grand finale of a white dog mess majestically impregnated with the stars and stripes.

Every single dog crap along that sidewalk had been claimed for the United States of America. 'A small step for a man...' etc... 'Do not ask what your country can do for you...' etc.

And once back at home I sat in front of my fire, coffee in hand, and reflected upon what I had just seen. I thought about the person who would unfortunately always remain anonymous to me, who had gone to the effort of making and planting all those little flags in order that I, and others following the same route, would have a smile on our faces that day. Somebody, somewhere, had this amusing idea and, even more commendably, saw it through.

------•••------

Thanks to that person I was given a day that I have not forgotten... And which returns to me even now... even... odds... tails you lose. On the roulette wheel of life I always bet on green. Even now...

------•••------

Um - I recall smiling and tossing a magazine onto the seat next to me. Where was that? It was late summer; I remember it feeling like the end of warmth was imminent. That's right – I was returning to Oxford having spent a week with my parents in my hometown in southwest Wales, where I left my car. That's it... I was, I was... yeah, on a bus... on a coach. That's it; I'm on a coach... The lights at the back are flickering – that's it, it was difficult to read I think. Yes, the lights were flickering – probably a bulb needed changing...

The countryside rolled by and the Severn Bridge came and went... I had returned to Britain from Portugal in late June. But I wanted to get to Berlin and out of the UK before the winter set in. From the end of October to March Britain was neither crisp nor mild, it was drizzly grey. I did not mind cold, it was the damp I hated. Portugal with its temperate climes had been fine. And I had taken full advantage of its location by spending a couple of crazy weeks over Christmas in Morocco and Gibraltar.

But I'd been ready for a change. I remember wanting to leave Portugal – despite its sun and beauty. And possibly that was stupid, and I should have stayed put. As far as I remember that wasn't what I did though. No – I'd gone to live in Oxford for a while before moving to Berlin. That's right, I'd gone back to Blighty to spend another summer in Oxford – with a one-week holiday with my parents in Wales.

And then after Oxford I'd needed to get away again. The weather was naturally an important consideration. But the other reason I needed to leave was because of a baffling two month relationship I had in Oxford with a girl named Caroline…

------•••------

I feel as though I'm lying on the floor of a Russian forest, staring up through the gap in the trees at the clouds and the blue. And the light spirals around high up and far away, and the trees represent some dark force on the peripheries of my vision and of my thoughts… And I sense that I have been stretched out here for both a thousand years and no time at all. The light flickers and is gone, and all that remains is the imprint of the silhouetted tree-shadows like sorcerers' fingers on the insides of my lids.

------•••------

Nobody knew I was returning. I simply turned up at the door of my old lodgings unannounced. But since no one was in, I went round to the back of the house and prised open the window of what had been my room. It had always had a dodgy latch.

I threw my rucksack in first and climbed in. The door to my room, however, had been locked on the outside; I had never locked it in my days. So any ideas I had had of going to the kitchen and making my first cup of British tea and slices of marmite on toast in a year, I had to put on hold.

The room smelled sweet: dhoop sticks and girlie things. On the white door, which led to the hallway, was an oblong of black card with silver gothic writing that read: *She was a good egg who made awful omelettes...* The bed was a large single mattress on the floor in the corner of the room. Three feet above the pillow was a bookshelf. Next to the bed were two orange painted fruit boxes. One had one of those 70s metal desk lamps on it, the ones with the flexi stalks. The other had a double cassette deck ghetto blaster on it. The line of tapes in front of the stereo had quite probably, at one time, been neatly arranged. Now, like the books on the bookshelf, one end of the line had tilted and toppled over.

In the diagonally opposite corner to the bed was a desk strewn with papers, pens, and an open file. Above the desk was a cork notice board, full of notes and phone numbers and a photograph of five people smiling on a beach in the sun. Two of the walls had North African rugs on them. The ceiling was covered in a pale blue and white striped billowing material, which I later found out was a parachute. There were three pictures on the wall next to the bed. One was of Tom Waits; one was of five moustached men wearing what were probably nineteenth century clothes, with the inscription 'The Haymarket Tragedy'; and the third picture was a pencil drawing of a woman with spiky hair.

It was early evening, and because of my late last night before leaving Wales and the coach journey, I was exhausted. I slipped everything off except for my T-Shirt and boxer shorts. I crawled under the black duvet with a white hand-painted Ying and Yang symbol on it, onto the red sheet, and put my head on the sweet smelling pillow. I lay there for only ten seconds before reaching out for a cassette. I picked up the first one and placed it in the deck. I found the volume knob and turned it low. It was a self-made compilation tape.

I did not get much of a chance to assess the quality of the bedroom owner's compilation. For, soon after the beginning of the first track I slipped into one of those deep comatose sleeps... which is probably the closest thing we get to experiencing what death is really like.

I awoke with a warm body next to me.

"Morning," it said. "Sleep well?" And she immediately proceeded to 'skin one up'. And that was my first encounter with both Caroline and Mary-Jane.

It is not easy to explain all the nuances of the effects of smoking hashish to somebody who has never smoked it before. It is not like being drunk. Alcohol numbs the senses whereas hashish heightens them: the music Caroline played that first morning sounded great; the conversation was absorbing; I could not take my eyes away from a book she had about fractals; the love-making was intense; and we could not stop laughing at any and every thing. We laughed so much that the tears were rolling down our cheeks, our sides hurt, and my face ached from having a perpetual dentist cat's grin plastered all over it.

She told me that finding a strange man in her bed had not fazed her. She'd heard a lot about me from the other tenants, and seen photos of me on their walls.

That first evening I took her to the foreign film cinema where I had spent so much time prior to my departure for Portugal. She took me to the Pitt Rivers museum the following day. I cooked her Mexican food, and she made me curry... She had not been in Oxford long – she had only been in my old room for two and a half weeks prior to my turning up.

I introduced her to my friends and fell in love. We smoked pot every day, went to bed in the early hours, and got up late. I signed on and she happily got to know the town before her term started. She was going to be doing an MA in something to do with language. It was along the lines of Linguistics, or The History of Language, although the exact title escapes me now... My English Language Teaching, and my general interest in the communication between people, meant that I felt I could hold my own in any such subject-related conversations. Why I felt a need to impress her with my knowledge of the English language, when it was she who was going to be doing the course, I can only surmise was because I liked her so much.

We would marvel at the illogical beauty of English, and at how truly multi-influenced it was... I recall Caroline telling me that French and Italian, unlike English, had Academies that would arbitrate over any language issues that might arise; such as which new words should be allowed into the language. She told me, however, that this easy-flowing naturally evolving language of ours had itself, at times, experienced pressures to have a governing body rule over it. She opened one of her text books that she'd got in preparation for her course, and told me that in the second half of the 16th Century Daniel Defoe called for there to be an English Language Academy, stating that it should be "...as criminal to coin words as to coin money"; and Jonathan Swift saw "...no absolute necessity why any language should be perpetually changing."

We agreed that it was the English language's free spirit, anarchic nature, and unshackled liberty that made it such a constant joy. English evolves; words come and go…

------•••------

And this is the way my brain is at the moment. Words and memories flowing in and out. Something similar to pollen on the wind, drifting around and swept away, and then settling on something both familiar and new.

------•••------

I remember us looking up weird and wonderful words. Caroline's favourite was crytoscopophilic, which is 'the urge to look through the windows of the houses you pass'. And I seem to recall that my favourite of all was sesquipedalian, which means 'long and complicated words'.

This, I suppose, was our bizarre method of preparing Caroline for her course. She was anxious. She had been to some non-descript provincial University to do her Bachelor's degree. Due to hard work, excellent grades, and some good fortune, she had been offered a place at Oxford. But she was not sure if she was up to it. Her early arrival in Oxford was to help her to get to know the place, and to enable her to work through her preparatory reading list.

And so it was. We would wake up and get stoned, drink coffee and chat. Then Caroline would go and spend a few hours in the library or Blackwell's bookshop, or both. And I would go for a walk along the river, or to the Botanical Gardens, or to sign on. About twice a week I too would go to the library, get a book out and spend the afternoon reading in a sunny beer garden. In the evening, we would eat, occasionally go to one of our local pubs, and then go home to smoke hashish and tell each other what we'd done that day, and what new knowledge we'd acquired that related to Caroline's course.

And, I did not mind in the slightest. If all this was helping Caroline's preparation and confidence, I was all for it.

------•••------

And now… now… those times come back to me like a doppelganger's dream, clear and vivid, and full of double meaning. And I still feel cold, even in the glow of the sunshine of yesterday's recollections.

------•••------

My friends were beginning to make noises about not seeing much of me. I had been away in Portugal for a year, and now that I was back – well, they could not tell the difference, so they told me… They had a point.

We did not just get stoned and talk about language, Caroline and I. We would also discuss politics and philosophy; and listen to reels and reels of cassettes. And I recall how I liked to think of it as my 'Summer of Tongue'…

One particular evening I remember I didn't have much to contribute to the conversation. And I felt, probably foolishly, I had let her down. So I vowed to come up with something really good to impress her with the following day.

"Our language" I began recounting from the sheets of paper I had scrawled notes onto that following afternoon while in the library, "is a heterogeneous tongue, composed as it is of words that have been influenced by, and evolved out of, all the miscellaneous peoples and events that have shaped the history of these islands off the West coast of Europe. And," I continued, "of the myriad influences that have sculpted the language, there have been three main sources…" Caroline bent down and put a Tom Waits tape into the deck. And as she did so, I told her that the three major linguistic influences on English had been "Primitive Germanic; Latin (and its descendants); and Greek." I told her, "Primitive Germanic – is the father of German, Dutch, the Scandinavian languages, and Yiddish… Latin – and its children, the Romance languages, has been an enormous influence on our tongue… and, Greek indirectly influenced English through Latin; the fact, however, that most of our scientific and medical terminology comes from Greek shows that it has also had a more direct influence."

I flicked the page over and Caroline listened intently as I told her: "It is believed that Celtic was the first Indo-European language to have been spoken in the British Isles in around 2000 BCE… A few hundred years later the Norsemen invaded Britain; then we experienced our first ever common currency when we became an outpost of the Roman Empire – during the first century CE… In the fifth and sixth centuries," I went on, "after the demise of the Romans, the Angles; the Saxons; and the Jutes – who came from the North Sea region – brought their language of Olde English to Britain."

I don't know why, but Caroline made me think of an intelligent duck. Possibly it was her lips, which were more protruding than pouting. Whatever it was, I found her attractive… Her face was the shape of an inverted rounded-off at the edges triangle. She had slightly rosy cheeks; her hair was jaw-line in length, straight, and mousy-brown. Her eyes often had this far away look to them, and were walnut brown in colour.

I lifted my eyes from the sheets in my hand and looked across the room to where Caroline was sitting. She smiled a smile that only affected the corner of one side of her mouth, and reached over for her red-tinted rectangular-framed glasses.

"And, by the way," I said, "Olde English lasted until a little after the Norman Conquest of 1066…"

"I *know* when the Norman invasion was," she said with a look I hadn't seen before. It was a cross between indignation and I suppose something akin to spitefulness.

"Yeah, I'm sure you do. I didn't mean anything… I was just saying… Look," I said with a slight shake of the head, "er… shall I continue?"

"Yes, it's very interesting," she said with her head tilted to one side.

"So, erm, yeah, the, er, power and high office that the French enjoyed in Britain meant that their tongue had a great influence on our language. So much so that two to three hundred years after their invasion Olde English was virtually unrecognisable. The Middle English period, however, from…"

"1150-1500," interjected Caroline.

"Yeah… witnessed the decline of the effects of French on the peoples here; who after all, during the 100 Years War were the enemy."

Caroline picked a magazine off the floor and placed it on her knees. "'Nother joint?" she said.

I nodded, and with an over-whelming sense of self-satisfaction at how much better I'd 'performed' this night than on the previous night, I decided to quickly finish off what I'd copied down in the library earlier that day.

"After this," I said, "well, what was in fact a series of wars and not one single 116 year war, and after the influence that the Bubonic Plague had on the language – wiping out about an eighth of the population – from the early 1500s we start to see the appearance of what we would be able to recognise as standard English… Nearly finished."

"Oh, you take your time, *lurrv*." This I found odd. She had said 'oh you take your time' in the most upper-crusted and refined manner. Whereas, she had emitted the 'lurrv' in a high pitched, back of the throat, screech – like some fag-ash trawler fishwife. Somewhat unsettled, I smiled and attempted to look her in the eye. But her red-tinted shades, coupled with the scarf draped over the light, which created an orange glow that permeated the room, did not allow me to see whether she was joking or not.

I tentatively stumbled another couple of sentences out. About the fact that if we add a sprinkling of Australian soap operas, the influence of mass-communication, and the IT revolution – we more or less have our version of standard English: 'new-millennium speak'.

Caroline was sneering. "Very good. Very interesting," she said sarcastically.

I did not get it. What had I done wrong? Surely, this was good not bad. I had spent several hours in the library researching and précising the history of the English language for her. OK, I was uncertain how much of it she already knew. But nevertheless, informative or not, I thought it would re-emphasise how eager I was to help her in her run up to being an Oxford student, which I knew she found to be a daunting prospect. And because I'd felt she'd been a little distant over the previous few days, I figured this would reignite her interest in me.

She stood up from her desk chair where she had been passively sitting the whole while. She reached under her knee-length black skirt with her free hand and wriggled off her underwear, which I noticed were a pair of my boxer shorts. She dropped onto all fours and prowled over to me in slow motion like a big cat. Half way through her diagonal route over to where I was sitting on the bed, she paused to simulate a snarl at the same time as reaching out in my direction and clawing at the air. Ash fell to the carpet from the smoking joint in her hand, and I forced a weak smile in her direction. But, she would not make eye contact with me.

On reaching my feet, she held out the joint ensuring that her averted gaze did not cross my line of vision. I reached out and began to lightly stroke her hand. But she was not having any of it, and snatched it away as soon as it was apparent that I was not taking the joint from her... She made another clawing motion in my direction, this time accompanied by a hiss. Then she thrust her hand towards me once again, this time urgently wagging the joint at me. I took it, and she made a 'humph' noise... She placed her left hand on my knee and the hand that had held the joint she put on my crotch. I put my hand gently but firmly on hers. She pushed it aside and began to unzip me. Once again, I put my hand on hers, a little more firmly this time. But she bent my middle finger back. So, I gave up.

I sat there not really knowing what to do. In the time I had known her, she had never behaved like this. Admittedly, we had not known each other long, but it had been intense from the outset. We had slept together before I had even known her name – and we had lived together from day one. Maybe it was a reaction. Maybe she was mirroring the way she felt I had treated her. Possibly she had seen my – admittedly slightly self-congratulatory – history of English as being patronising or belittling to her. Or, she may have seen my enthusiastic speech as aggressively attempting to affirm my intellectual superiority over hers... And, if that was how she saw things, it was clearly now my turn to be the submissive one. And so I remained silent and let her get on with it.

She clumsily fished around for my floppy penis, trying to slip it through the top of the opening in my boxer shorts where two of my buttons were missing. She soon aborted this manoeuvre, however, and began to undo the remaining buttons on my shorts. Once she'd undone the final button, she put my considerably unexcited organ in her mouth. And then, through the corner of her mouth, she told me to: "Say sorry."

"What?"

"Say sorry," she growled as she tightened her teeth around my penis.

And since I didn't think she was joking, I said, "I'm really sorry Caroline," with as sincere a voice as I could muster up... Fortunately, at this point the doorbell rang, which, added to my enforced apology, led her to soften her grip. As soon as I felt her teeth were retracted, I said: "Maybe I should answer that."

"No, leave it," she said as the bell began to ring again.

"I really better get it, there might not be anyone else in."

"But," she began, "I wanted to do this for you." She took her mouth from around my penis, and looked up at me pleadingly.

"Maybe later, yeah?" I said, but not fucking likely, I thought, as I tidied myself up.

I went barefoot into the threadbare landing and opened the door. It was Rachid, who had come round to see if anything exciting was going on. "Hey man what's happening?" he asked.

"Hi Rach – not much."

IX

Rachid was a hair-extensioned hippy of Algerian descent. His parlance was a mixture of a 60s West Coast Joplin-esque drug twang, and geek-ish freak speak…

Everybody loved Rachid. He was someone who would do anything to help anyone – no matter what it involved, and irrespective of whether he was any help or not.

Rachid always had a plastic carrier bag with him. But it was never any old familiar plastic bag; it always had some cool psychedelic or retro design on it. Jez, who lived in the room above mine, or rather above Caroline's, thought that Rach made them himself, or at least the prints on them. I was not so sure, but they certainly were pieces of art. They were often designs for shops that no one had ever heard of. The bag he had with him on this particular visit had Andy Warhol's picture of Chairman Mao on it. And, in bubble writing underneath the picture was written: 'Warhol's! For Clothes With Holes.'

In his plastic bags he always had a variety of miscellaneous items; but, as far as anyone could tell, cassettes, a notepad, and a music magazine were always in permanent residence.

"Jez and Skinny in man?"

"Everybody's out except for me and Caroline."

"Um… OK if I hang out for a bit?"

"Do you fancy coming for a couple of pints?"

"No bread man, you dig."

"I'll get you a couple Rach."

"Um. The old lady coming?" I shook my head. "OK... yeah man, let's do it."

I went to get my jacket and tell Caroline what I was doing. She didn't reply, she merely nodded and smiled. She at least had the decency, I thought, to look a bit sheepish – sitting in the corner of the bed with her back against the wall and her arms hugging her knees. As I was leaving the room she said, "Have fun."

"Thanks," I replied.

Then very timidly she said: "Er, what year did the... er, hundred year war start?"

"Um... 1337, I think I remember reading... something like that."

"Oh yeah, right, thanks... Bye."

"Yeah, see you later."

"OK. Maybe I'll make something nice for us to eat for when you get back..."

But I'd turned and was closing her bedroom door when she said this, so I didn't bother replying.

Rach and I walked down the road considering where to go. A group called Café Puschkin were playing at The Adelphi, so we decided not to go there. Not because we didn't like them, but we just wanted a quiet drink... We turned right at the next corner and Rachid waved to some girl with shoulder length bright red hair. Then we crossed the road and went into The Barrel Organ. Rach found a place in the corner by the pool table, while I bought us a couple of pints of Bitter. Once I'd come over with our drinks we played three frames of pool before finally sitting down to have a chat.

Rachid threw back the final two fingers of his beer, and I asked him if he fancied another pint. But he opted instead for half a pint of Bitter in a pint glass and a bottle of Newcastle Brown… As I placed our tray of drinks on the table the cue ball flew over and hit Rach on the knee. He shouted "Ouch!" and rubbed his knee vigorously. The lanky early twenty-something guy with the ginger hair, and the battle going on between freckles and acne for facial dominance, apologised for his ebullient break. Magnanimous as always Rachid reassured him that it was really no problem at all, and "accidents happen." And this guy who had just given two shots away, picked up the white ball from under the table behind us and placed it into his friend's hand…

That evening I told Rachid about the whole Caroline saga – everything from the first night to the moment when Rachid had rung the doorbell. I recounted how into each other I thought we had been. Rachid listened and nodded, smiled and tutted at what he deemed to be the appropriate moments.

I told him that until about a week before, we had been getting on fine – but then Caroline had gradually become more distant. Then I paused, waited, and observed the concerned look on Rachid's face. And I leaned back in my chair as he gazed with a furrowed brow at the matchstick-thin roll-up he was rolling. He nodded almost imperceptibly – the resultant punctuation to a concluded internal dialogue, I presumed.

He let out a sigh and said: "Yeah, man."

"Well, what do you think Rach?"

"Yeah… well, you know – like is it my place to say, you dig?"

"Of course it is Rach. I'm asking for your opinion."

"Yeah, cool, I know man… but do you want it as it is, or sugar-coated?"

"I want the truth Rach. I want you to tell me what you think."

"OK. Strap yourself in friend, it might be a bumpy ride… you dig?"

I obviously did not 'dig' at all. For what I was expecting was a commentary on the incidents I had just recounted to Rachid – and not, well not, what he proceeded to tell me. And that was that he could not think of anyone who liked Caroline. It was more than simply being impassive towards her, people really *did not* like her. According to Rachid, I had been back for nearly the whole Summer and yet had hardly seen any of my old friends. Apparently, people had been looking forward to seeing me again once they heard that I'd returned from Portugal. But I had just spent the whole time wrapped up with Caroline.

Apart from the one or two token drinks with friends in the first couple of weeks of being back, that had been it. Initially people had phoned the house and left messages with Caroline. But after a while, when I had not bothered returning their calls, they had given up on me. I told Rach that I had not got any messages. And Rach looked me straight in the eyes with a 'What does that tell you?' look on his face.

And because of what Rachid saw as her duplicitous central column, he had taken a strong disliking to her. He'd taken a disliking to her ways and the manner in which she pretended to be one thing when in reality she was something completely different. She professed to believe in equality and care about the underdog when, according to Rachid, the truth was that she was out for what she could get. Rachid concluded by saying he found her to be two-faced, and the second face she kept well hidden from me…

When I returned later that evening she'd gone. Her holdall and rucksack, and her clothes from the wardrobe, had disappeared. And later, when I had stopped feeling shocked and the numbness had passed, I searched for a clue or a sign as to why she had left without saying a word. She hadn't even left me a note, and it's funny what travels through the portals of the mind when all one has is nuance and memories.

And so I searched for something to say about it all – but the conversations I kept having had no listener. It was too late; it is *too late*… And, as is the wont of the perturbed mind, I wondered if the scraps of paper on her desk, or the pictures on the wall, might hold a clue. At times like these, one finds meaning in the smallest of things. And despite feelings to the contrary, I had to remind myself that I was not lost in an episode of Columbo; and the moment for a raised finger and a final searching question had long gone.

And, much later, once in the comfort of my own solitude, I allowed myself to be sidetracked into considering whether the picture of 'The Haymarket Tragedy' on Caroline's wall might shine any halogen clarity onto the workings of her mind:

On the evening of May 4th 1886, a group of anarchists met to plan a demonstration in response to violence that had erupted during a strikers' rally at the McCormick Reaper Works in Chicago earlier that day.

The demonstration, or rather as it tuned out the mass meeting, began at 20.30h... As the gathering was drawing to a close at 22.00h, 176 policemen heavy-handedly moved in demanding that the 200 remaining workers should go home. Without warning a bomb went off, shortly followed by police fire – and possibly return fire from workers. Sixty policemen were injured and seven eventually died. Later, medical reports showed that most of the police injuries were caused by shots from their own guns. It was never found out how many workers died or were injured.

Over the next few days, all the prominent Socialists and Anarchists were rounded up. Eight of them ended up being tried. They were convicted (and the court's decision was subsequently upheld by both the Illinois Supreme Court and later the US Supreme Court) for "inflammatory speeches and publications" which directly led to the riotous behaviour of the gathering.

On the 11th November 1887, four of the eight were hanged, two were given life sentences, one committed suicide whilst in prison, and one remained locked up despite there being no case against him.

Shortly after the election of a new Governor in 1893, all were pardoned. The Governor stated that the jury had specifically been chosen to convict the men, and that it would have been impossible to have a fair trial under such a prejudiced and un-objective judge...

A commemorative monument to the tragedy and travesty was erected in Haymarket Square in 1889. In 1890 somebody tried to blow it up. A year later it was moved to a nearby park because it was deemed to be a danger to road users. In early summer 1903 the

State crest and city seal were stolen from it. In 1927 a driver drove straight into it stating that he could not stand the sight of it any longer. A year later, in 1928, after extensive repair work was completed, it was moved from the edge of the park to nearer the middle.

Then, exactly thirty years to the day later, on May 4th 1958, it was moved again – this time to by the road, only 200 feet from its original site. In 1969, a bomb exploded at the foot of the statue. In November of the same year – after having been once again restored – black ink was thrown all over it. After another bomb went off at its base in 1970, the then Mayor placed a twenty-four hour guard on it. When, in 1972, it was judged to be too expensive to keep a police presence constantly at the site, it was moved to police headquarters… And, in October 1976 the monument was yet again moved – this time to the police academy, where it can be viewed only by prior arrangement…

Um… Interesting though it was, it didn't reveal anything about the inner workings of Caroline's mind. Nothing I didn't already know.

I remember sporadically keeping in touch with my Oxford friends. I recall asking them if they had had any sightings of Caroline. None of them had, which I found odd. Oxford is not *such* a large town, and I would have expected someone to have bumped into her in a pub, or seen her shopping in town, or something. But, no…

My next thought was that possibly she had left altogether. I had found that hard to believe at first, what with her impending course. Then I remembered that Caroline had never shown me any proof she'd been accepted onto a course. All I'd ever had was her word – good enough under normal circumstances… Or, I considered, maybe she had got a transfer to another University.

Oh, the permutations were incalculable. And, not only was it a waste of time interpreting all the possibilities and shades of meaning, it was also pointless.

People do not neatly fit into painstakingly chiselled away boxes. People are unpredictable, they do things out of character, and they react inconsistently, and act in ways that later even *they* cannot explain...

You may even arrive at a satisfactory conclusion as to why a person acted in a certain way, which momentarily gives you peace of mind. But it is not a steadfast and untroubled peace of mind. It is a peace of mind based upon judgements; judgements often to make you feel better about yourself.

And reluctantly I had to accept that I would never know why Caroline had acted as she had. Nor whether there had been any moment when Caroline had felt for me the way I had felt about her...

X

*A*nd I feel how Lee Harvey Oswald's defence lawyer would have felt. And I feel I'm in a bubble, that I'm in pain – but I'm not. No, it's not that. It's being on a cusp, or in a song title that refers to something just out of reach… that refers to a climate of understanding that one is not quite privy to… It's out of order and I'm under starters orders.

And I feel like Marilyn Monroe's best friend, or James Dean's mechanic; Marc Bolan's postman, or Olga Corbett's first judge. I don't really know what identity means any longer. And who I have become is wound around the extended finger of time, and is mounted on a plaque inscribed with a timeline depicting my life. My life: my past, my now-time, and my future.

And I have no idea what I am supposed to do with my knowledge… with my knowledge… with my lack of remembrance I believe I mean. But like Ben Johnson's moral compass, I have forced myself into some form of totalitarian denial – where truth is lies, and I can no longer rely upon myself to distinguish what is what. And something keeps irritating me and interrupting my thoughts… possibly it's a fluctuating temperature thing. Huh – I don't know, maybe it's a fluctuating me – maybe I'm coming down with something; maybe I'm coming down with something more than just forgetfulness.

------•••------

It was always good to return home to southwest Wales, especially after having been out of the country for a while. Home was a little fishing village that nestled in the midst of a region awash with Norman Castles, Celtic Mythology, and desolate beaches.

My earliest memory is of the whole family sitting transfixed in front of my grandparents' black and white tele. And my grandfather turning to me and in his 30-a-day Welsh timbre saying: "Try and remember this bach, it's very important."

It was 1969, and we were watching the moon landing... Years later, not a tossed rock away from what subsequently became my parents' house, in a local Inn, I recall being told a story about the moon landing. I believe it was an old poacher who told me the story, or it could have been the person who'd been sitting next to him at the bar. It all seems so long ago now. And, for whatever reason, the story has rushed like a silver bullet to the fore of my mind. And as with the poster on Caroline's wall, and the things she said, I'm not sure if it holds any significance. I'm not sure if it will tell me what is happening to me... or what my name is.

It is merely a story, like many others – like the one I should have written... Like the one I should have written, which might have resembled this, these thoughts, these asides, these skewed night-time drive-time anecdotal snippets. Had I got round to it, this both subdued and monumental reaching out for meaning could have been where my story began... or where it ended.

For a short period while Neil Armstrong was walking on the moon, the sound being broadcast to television sets all over the planet was lost. This technical hitch, however, was not experienced at NASA Head Quarters... And it was during this time when Neil Armstrong muttered to himself the words, "Good Luck Mr Bolovski."

After he had returned to earth and been de-briefed, and gone through whatever an astronaut has to go through, he was asked what "Good luck Mr Bolovski" meant. But he just shrugged it off as meaning not very much at all. Over the years, however, he was often asked who Mr Bolovski was, and why he had wished him luck. But he was always reluctant to answer, saying that it was not important. To which he was reminded that every utterance he had made was significant, since it had been made on the moon.

The story I remember being told in that little pub in south Wales was that many years later, on meeting a former colleague in a bar, after a few drinks, Neil Armstrong finally recounted the significance of his words: 'Good Luck Mr Bolovski.'...

On one occasion when Neil Armstrong was a boy, he was playing ball in his garden. He heard raised voices coming from next door. On peering over the fence, he saw Mr Bolovski, his next-door neighbour, skulking around the flowerbeds. Mrs Bolovski, still in her nightgown, was shouting out of the bedroom window at him: "Oral sex! Oral sex! I'll give you oral sex when... when... when that boy next door walks on the moon."

But here and now, with spinning forms and thoughts like frosted glass, I question whether the Americans ever landed on the moon in '69. I am flooded by recollections that help me little... I remember that up until 1969 the Americans had constantly been second best to the Soviet Union in the Space Race. The Soviets had the first dog in space, Laika. They had the first man in space, Yuri Gagarin. They had the first manned shuttle to orbit the earth; and they put the first woman in space, Valentina Tereshkova.

During this entire period, the Americans had been playing catch-up. And, though they were not ready for a manned trip to the moon they knew they had to do something quick or the Soviet Union would win that race too. Communism was succeeding over the mighty Capitalist Empire; 'evil was prevailing over good'. The Americans were not sure how advanced the Soviet Union was in its programme, but they knew they had to act quickly. Especially since President Kennedy had promised that America would put a man on the moon by the end of the 60s. Hence, so the argument goes, the US faked it.

I seem to recall that those who argue that the US never landed on the moon state that there are many anomalies for which NASA have never given any explanations...

Some of the photographs show the existence of additional lighting having been used, but no such lighting was supposed to have been used. Also, as Buzz Aldrin is climbing down the ladder onto the moon surface, there is a photograph that shows his boot being lit from below, which surely cannot be possible. Additionally, there are a series of photos taken by one astronaut of the other, which although we can see the reflection of the astronaut who is taking the photo holding his camera at chest height, the photograph has clearly been taken from above eye-level.

I believe there was also something concerning some of the photographs being at variance with the TV camera footage of the same events. Some of the wide-angle photographs show the shadows pointing in many different directions. And when NASA was asked how the films were protected from the intense cosmic radiation, they replied that the cameras had been painted with a coat of aluminium paint. But surely that would never have been sufficient.

According to the disbelievers, the most compelling evidence for the US having faked the whole lunar expedition is to do with the sound: when the astronauts are asked questions from the control room at Cape Canaveral their replies are instantaneous. Now, even with today's technology, when one is watching a news broadcast and the reporter is in, say, Palestine, it takes him one or two seconds to reply to the questions posed to him. So in 1969, from the moon? Surely, one would expect quite a substantial delay between the question being asked on earth and the reply returning from space.

I do not think I was swayed by one camp more than the other; it is only now that I doubt everything... And I am not sure why this comes to me now... All that appears to be gaining momentum in my distracted mind is how much more satisfying it would be if my first memory of this planet, as I sat there with my grandfather, was truly based upon mankind's first experience of another planet... And I wonder what my last recollection will be.

My father, my father. I remember my father. He's dead now. At least I believe he is... I recollect how he went through a phase of wearing a monocle. Sometimes weeks would go by without my mother or I seeing the dreaded thing. Then we would all go out somewhere, Sunday lunch in the pub down the village springs to mind. And we would each take a menu and begin to peruse it for something that appealed. My father would ceremoniously extract his monocle from his baggy trouser pocket. And my mother and I would cringe as we watched him squinting tightly in an attempt to grip the thing by tensing up the muscles around his eye. It would drop out a couple of times, but after a while he managed to achieve some kind of precarious hold on the eye-piece – just so long as he kept his free eye shut... But after a spate of frequent usage my father's eye became blood-shot. And we never saw it again after that.

My father was a historian. He had been at the Nuremberg War Trials as part of the French contingency, and had been involved in some of the French Resistance's operations.

The French Resistance was a badly organised well-intentioned amalgamation of many different anti-Nazi groups... I recall him telling me that on one occasion he was given instructions by the Resistance to go and dig himself a cave in a particular range of hills, and to take enough tinned food with him to last three or four weeks. He had been told that the war was coming to an end, and soon the Nazis would be retreating. His job, along with others, was to 'cut them off at the pass' so to speak... My father never carried out these instructions – which was fortunate, for had he done so he would have been in that cave for nearly two years. It was 1943.

Another time, my father had to travel across occupied France. He happened to mention this to his Uncle. And as much *en passant* as anything else my father told him that he required false papers. His Uncle immediately offered to get them for him at a considerably lower price than was the norm. I remember my father telling me that it was not a run of the mill task getting forged papers; you needed the correct paper, the correct stamps, and the right signatures – or at least well-forged copies. And this could take an inordinately long time.

However, not only did his Uncle obtain the necessary documentation for considerably lower than the normal price, he also managed to obtain everything in double quick time... Meticulous planning and memorising of cover story complete, my father boarded the train that would take him through Nazi-controlled France. During this period there would be frequent random document checks, but my father was confident that he had the best forged papers that money could buy.

As my father sat idly watching the passing meadows and trees through the window, along with the four other strangers in his compartment, he felt the train pulling to an unscheduled halt. Looking out of the window, he saw German soldiers preparing to board.

Several minutes passed before two soldiers slid open the door and requested to see everybody's documentation. The four strangers in turn handed their papers to the two Nazis. They then approached my father who duly handed them the documents that his Uncle had acquired for him. In less than a minute the two soldiers were roaring with laughter. My father, with an anguished smile on his face, enquired as to what the joke was. He was told that his documentation was the worst example of forged papers they had ever come across.

Consequently, my father was carted off in a truck to a Prisoner of War Camp in Toulouse. Essentially, it was a pre-concentration camp camp, from where trainloads of prisoners would be shuttled off to the death camps in Germany.

My father was driven into the camp with an assortment of dodgy looking characters. They were all escorted to a room where they were told to drop their trousers. This was to establish if any of them were Jewish… Over the coming days, my father found it rather disconcerting that none of the other inmates wanted to talk to him… He later discovered that this was because he had been brought in with a lorry-load of pimps, drug dealers, and members of the underworld. And the others in the camp had assumed that my father was an equally unsavoury character, and consequently wanted nothing to do with him.

After having been incarcerated for less than a week, there was a roll call. All the inmates lined up in the yard and were addressed by the camp commander. They were told that the French Resistance had killed one of the top Nazis in the area. And until the perpetrators of this "atrocity against the fatherland" had either been brought to justice or had given themselves up, one person from the camp would be shot each day, beginning the following day with the youngest. My father, thinking that this was abhorrent, looked around and suddenly realised that he was the only one without substantial stubble on his face. And subsequently he was informed that he was the youngest and would be executed early the next morning by firing squad.

Thinking about all of this reminds me of how fortunate my father was not to be killed, and how like Damocles' sword this whole existence thing is... A combination of the allies advancing, and the Nazis either fleeing for Switzerland or wishing to be seen in a positive light by their captors, meant that my father was forgotten about. Not before, so I remember him recounting, he bizarrely had one of the best night's sleep he has ever had...

This goes against my understanding of such situations, however, and it used to leave me feeling uneasy, for, I surmised, if I were ever to find myself in a similar situation I'd be screaming with fear or scraping my nails down to the bone to get out of there.

Not that I have ever been in such a situation. Not an identical situation, or should I say not a situation whereby perceived imminent death has been thrust upon me... Oh, I don't know. I do somewhat dreamily remember the Dadaist who said at the age of 23 that he would kill himself at the age of 30, and did...

My father had been a naughty and high-spirited child. And as an adult it was occasionally apparent that he had a well-developed offbeat sense of humour and could often see the more absurd side of things. However, more common was a somewhat subdued inwardly looking person. And if it is possible to trace a person's character from the events they were involved in, then my father's experiences during the war certainly shaped the person he became. Without these experiences, my father may well have been a more boisterous soul, more true to the child that he was. But who knows?

It is quite probable that a contributory factor in my father having slept a deep uninterrupted sleep the night before he was going to be killed was his strong Catholic belief. It is quite possible that he came to terms with whatever he had to come to terms with, and made his peace with God... Whereas I am a non-believer, but I don't think that is a hindrance to my chances of... of... oh, I don't know, of dealing with my own demons and doubts I suppose.

A thought, a memory, from I don't know when, arrives like a skimmed stone through the rippled surface of my mind... I am on a train; I think it is the train that brought me to London. Yes, it must be because I can hear English being spoken... Oh – now I remember: I overheard somebody articulating their timely and, I thought, enlightened theory on death: that it is only atheists who will have an afterlife...

But yes – my father lived and I am *here* today.

XI

I reread the first few lines of the article on Berlin.

...Berlin is a city of cranes, trains, and men at work. A city sprinting headlong towards the future with its feet firmly planted in the past. It remains an island in a sea of history. A crossroads between past and present; old ideas and new trends; East and West; DDR and BRD. The West is the West and the East is racing to catch up. The new German capital is a city of flux; blink and you might miss something. A place deliciously ebbing and flowing with the tides of change.

On the opposite page was a brief history of Berlin from 1900, finishing off with a list about Berlin today:

In Berlin, according to the article, there are: –

1	Woman sentenced to life imprisonment;
3	People from Grenada;
4	People from the Vatican City;
6	People from Lichtenstein;
9	People from Tonga;

10	People from Malawi;
30	Sheep;
41	Penguins;
66	Pigs from Pankow;
77	Men with life sentences;
111	People who became orphans during World War II;
123	People with dysentery;
143	Urine and Bladder Doctors;
161	Suspected poachers;
644	Employees in Ice-cream shops;
749	Men from Thailand;
865	Homeless people under 18;
1999	Members of Judo Clubs;
2000	Workers of the Foreign Office;
3000	Social Services Department workers;
4200	Berlin citizens who are requesting the Mayor's help with something;
4242	Females from Thailand;
7389	Australians;
8800	Berliners born on 24th December;
15,732	Chickens;
137,109	Turkish people;
208,306	School children;
337,484	People on social security benefits;
2,997,383	Germans.

I sat next to Barry on the flight to Berlin; an Irish guy in his late twenties who was going to look for work on one of the Berlin building sites… Barry and I ate our plastic airline food with our plastic cutlery. I told him it had probably been a Welsh man who had first discovered America, and he told me that he would not be surprised if he heard that an Irish man had first set foot on the moon.

He told me that his grandfather was the stationmaster of a small station in the back of beyond in County Mayo. During the summer a Swiss fresh air type in his late fifties, with sturdy hiking boots and trousers tucked into his thick all-weather socks, complained that the clocks at either end of the station were displaying different times. Barry's grandfather told him that there would be no point in having two clocks if they both told the same time.

------•••------

Time rushes by like a Japanese bullet train. And I wish I had a clock or a watch-piece, maybe one that hangs on a chain – all elegant and accurate. For I wish I knew if it was day or night… fight or flight, which would allow me to sing to the morning light.

And I know I have memories, and concentration is somehow good… And these are the memories that make me… er, me. Tigers padding around, the clearing mist, and the smell of baking bread – whirlwind swallows on currents of air; and a million cups of tea. Go on, go on, go on. I shall go on – until I reach the end… Won't we all.

------•••------

We landed in Berlin's Schönefeld airport, the smaller of the capital's two main airports. The train station is on its doorstep, and I recall catching a train to the central station where I found a wooden bench, sat down, and thought about what to do next. I inhaled the freshly ground mid-morning coffee aromas that percolated in the air around me. And, deeming it as good an idea as any, I purchased a coffee and lit a cigarette.

I opened my guidebook and searched for inspiration… One of a troupe of three vagabonds came over to ask me for one of my cigarettes. He was the most clean-shaven and youngest of the three of them. The other two being bushy-bearded, cinematically classic images of what tramps should look like.

I remember wondering how they came to find themselves in their present situation, and I questioned why they did not make the trek down south. Surely the warmer weather would make their outdoor existence a little easier. Why don't the beaches of southern France, Italy, and Spain have more winter-migrating *clochards* sunning themselves – especially since there are no border controls nowadays?

I bought them each a beer and they came and sat at my table. One of older ones began talking to me. He reached into his inside pocket, and produced a tattered weather-beaten photograph of a youngish man in uniform with a bugle in his right hand. This was his son, I remember him recounting, of whom he was very proud. The manner in which he talked about the young man, with a watering eye, made me sad. And as I listened, I mused over whether it really was his son, and if it was, if he knew how much his father felt for him. And what had happened to the mother?

I felt a wave of melancholia drip-feed into me from a tube inserted into my arm. The obvious pride and love this man had for his son seemed somewhat misplaced. For, surely, if the son's feelings had been only half that of his father's he would not have let this happen.

At that moment the waitress came out to shoo them away like naughty little children or pre-house-trained puppies. They began to get up, but I told them to stay; and told her that they were with me and had not finished their drinks yet. She was not pleased, stomping off mumbling something about them finishing their drinks quickly and departing.

The youngest of the three, who looked to be in his late thirties, then proceeded to tell me his story. He told me that he had had a good job, a pretty wife, and a nice house in a nice street. He had returned home from work one day, poured himself a large whisky and sat down to vegetate in front of the television. And he sat there, and he sat there… and then he wriggled and eased himself out of his lizard skin and floated horizontally to the ceiling.

And in this out of body state, he gazed down upon himself. And a singular realisation engulfed him, which produced a silent internalised scream, as he saw himself watching TV programmes about other nice people living in other nice parts of towns doing nice things in nice houses... He descended back through the zip-up rear of his head and blinked his way back into his usual frame of consciousness. He looked round the room at cushions and flower prints, got out of his comfortable chair, slung some things into a bag and left. And has not been back since... He told me that he had felt like a prisoner in his own prison.

The waitress then reappeared, this time with the manager. On seeing them approaching, the vagabonds got up and in turn shook my hand. I wished them luck, and then they were gone.

------•••------

These recollections make me want to cough, but the phlegm won't come.

------•••------

XII

I took the remnants of my coffee and stood in the passageway. I stared out of the window and marvelled at the sheer density of it all. All those people, all those lives – each one meaningful, each one significant to the actors who were playing out their roles.

I watched as we traversed outer London, and considered the inter-connectedness of it all. People whose lives overlapped with other people's lives; and those other people's lives overlapping with yet other people's lives. An endless procession of people, of information being exchanged, of paths crossing and of stories being told... It was a city of secrets, a city of misunderstandings and loneliness, and a city of isolation and bricks.

London was a city of barriers and walls and futility. And yet, it was also a place of forged friendships and community. Either you were drowned out by the deafening enormity of it all, or you were exhilarated by the part you played in its totality... London was a city of contradictions, differing perceptions, and sometimes broken dreams.

The announcer announced that we would shortly be arriving at our destination. I had not been to London for a long time; I had had no reason to... I stuck my arm out of the window, turned the handle and opened the door. I stepped onto the platform and put the strap of my shoulder bag over my head. I looked up and around me, trying to catch sight of a station clock. None was visible. I lengthened my strides to catch up with a woman who had got off the same train. She had tight flower print trousers on. Her bottom gave a slight yet perceptible bounce with each step she took. I pulled up along side.

"Excuse me, have you got the time?" I asked, and she turned and looked at me with her brown Oriental eyes. I perceived her stare to be that of a contented soul, one that nevertheless had not ceased asking questions. To the extent that had the opportunity arisen I felt she would have been prepared to tell me more than just the hour. Or, just maybe, this was all in my head… For surely it's not possible to know the mind of another.

She lifted her left hand and pushed back the sleeve of her un-tucked white shirt with her right, and told me the time. I thanked her. Her tangible expectancy, and what I perceived as readiness for a new story to unfold, made it difficult not to invite her for a coffee at one of the station's many uninspiring styrofoam cafés. I might have, but the train's tardiness meant that I did not.

I proceeded with purpose along the platform, leaving the exotic stranger behind. I stopped several metres shy of the ticket barrier and groped around for my one-way ticket in my trouser pockets. Then, after a couple of minutes of not finding it and thinking that possibly I'd mislaid it, I felt the flexible card that purported to be the most efficient means of recording the details of a train journey. It was sandwiched in the middle of my train timetable. I fingered the two entities apart and fished out the little card.

Along with my ticket, I also accidentally scooped out several coins that cascaded to the floor around my feet. As I bent down to pick up the scattered pieces of differing denominations I spotted one of the coins surreptitiously trying to make a break for it. I watched it roll its uneven path back along the platform. A foot came sharply down on it, squashing any idea it might have had of escaping to a better world where it's value would no longer solely be judged in terms of its buying power.

My gaze rose from the foot to the calf, up the familiar brightly coloured flower prints past the hips. I followed the white granddad shirt up past the bust and made eye contact with the owner of the foot. As she bent down and reached forward in slow motion, holding my gaze all the while, I thought about time. I thought about the time it was. I thought about the time I had. And I thought about how in a different place at a different time this pale-skinned beauty from the Orient would have reminded me of Lee Ying. But, this time – which was probably the only time – she did not...

And I felt kind of seasick, momentarily... for a moment. For the briefest moment in time, I felt as though the bright colours were drowning me out. Her bright coloured legs and the clothes of the passers-by were juxtaposed with my pallid thoughts and the pale skin of this woman bending before me. And as I bent, I briefly had a shoe-shiner's perspective – rushing thighs and callipered knee-joints; bodies severed at the waist, twitching towards the outside pavement light, to meet and pass other headless and faceless bodies. And I wished diamonds would cascade from the edge of the moon, in their hundreds and thousands – showing me the way towards bright hardened enlightenment... And then, like a village-hall-actor's double-take, with a rapid shake of the head I dispelled the cobwebs and the doubts, and sucked back in my aching reality...

I rose as she rose – some feathered mating dance with her jungle-wild legs. She placed the coin in my palm and said, "You could buy me a drink with that if you wanted." I did want, very much, but I simply could not. I explained that I would love to but that I was late, and I was in a hurry, and, and... And I just didn't have the time. And I knew that this was not a time for phone numbers. The time for phone numbers and phone calls was long gone. And, this certainly was not a time for 'what ifs?'

-------•••-------

I left my rucksack in luggage locker 12B. I threw the strap of my shoulder bag over my head and I headed down Kurfürstendamm, the Oxford Street of Berlin. It was not my thing; and just as Oxford Street is not typical of London, so Ku'damm, as it is known, is not typical of Berlin.

I was eager to get over to the former East part of the city. And as I ambled along in a vaguely easterly direction the sky bruised and it began to rain. I dashed into the first café I found. I took a window seat and waited for the waiter. After several minutes he arrived and I ordered a beer. Since none of the beers he mentioned meant anything to me, I asked him to give me a local brew... I sat there and watched as people ran to avoid the downpour, as a cornucopia of brollies sprouted like a plethora of multi-coloured fungi. And the beer tasted good even if one fifth of it was froth.

Across the road from the café that was keeping me dry, was an English Language School. Deciding that I might as well begin looking for a job immediately, I finished off my beer and popped into the toilet. I took off my black long-sleeved T-Shirt and switched it for a slightly crumpled white shirt. I put my T-Shirt into my bag and got out my mustard yellow tie. In the side pocket of my bag, along with my Olympus Trip camera, were folded photocopies of my qualifications and a couple of references. I threw a chewing gum into my mouth to take away the aroma of alcohol and returned to my table. I caught the waiter's attention and paid.

At the entrance of the school was a waste paper basket-cum-ashtray into which I discarded my spearmint-flavoured gum. I climbed the staircase to the first floor where I was greeted by the blindingly white grin of a secretary behind a counter. The school was called Beesleys. It was an international chain of schools. I knew it well; I had two friends who had worked for them in the past. Not in Berlin, but in two of its other centres.

It was an internationally known chain, but that did not necessarily make it a good place to learn foreign languages. In fact going by most chains in most fields it almost precluded it from being any good... Its approach to teaching languages, according to my friends who had worked for them, went against any modern internationally accepted methodologies of how foreign language learners should be taught. It also treated its employees terribly, and was very American in its outlook.

It was fast-food education: you might think you had been satisfied, but on closer inspection you had not got very much for your money, you had been treated ignorantly, you had probably played some part in the destruction of the rain forests, and you were still hungry. This was Beesleys down to a tee. It did not matter whether you were in one of their centres in Berlin or New York or Barcelona, their interiors were identical: all garish colours and metallic edges. Apparently, they had a buzzer that would sound every forty minutes. This buzzer was the same in each one of their centres the world over. It signified the end of class and the commencement of the five minute break.

Andrew, that was the name of my friend who had worked in their Frankfurt centre, told me that after working there a while he would give an anticipatory wince shortly prior to each time the buzzer was about to sound. It was similar to how some people wake up a minute before their alarm clock goes off – and as with Pavlov's dogs the buzzer signified when my friend could go out for a fag without getting electrocuted.

On one occasion, Andrew was taking a one-to-one class. The two of them were having a very interesting conversation; the student – a Director of a Frankfurt company – was expressing himself well, and using all the new English grammar that Andrew had been teaching him. The buzzer went off and Andrew, not wishing to halt the flow, asked his student if he wanted his five minute break immediately or after they had finished that particular topic. The student who was absorbed by what they were doing said he would rather wait a little while before taking the break. Ten minutes later the conversation came to its natural conclusion and they both went out for their respective coffees and cigarettes.

At the end of that day he got the most almighty of reprimands from the Head of the school. Andrew was told that it was irrelevant what he was in the middle of when the buzzer went off. When the buzzer sounded that was when everybody had to stop and take the five minute break. Even if a teacher was in the middle of a sentence, when the buzzer sounded that is when the break commenced – no exceptions...

In addition to their regimented approach to timekeeping, Beesleys had a very odd way of teaching languages, which they were unwarrantedly proud of. Their approach amounted to little more than learning parrot fashion... A teaching colleague of Andrew's told him that Beesleys bugged some of the classes to enable the Head of the school to listen in to ensure that the teachers were exclusively teaching the Beesleys Method. Andrew's colleague would arrive at class in the morning, take off her jacket, and throw it over the bug that she had discovered attached to the skirting board in the corner of her classroom.

To teach for Beesleys you did not need any teaching qualifications; you did not need any kind of qualifications whatsoever. You received a week's unpaid training, to assimilate their rather facile teaching methods...

The written word was completely ignored so as to concentrate uniquely upon speaking and listening. Beesleys Method for teaching new vocabulary, for example, was completely patronising. And was embarrassing for teacher and student alike – especially if either had had prior experience of other schools and other teaching methods.

Say, for example, the word to be taught was 'pen'. You, as the teacher (T), would begin by 'introducing' the new item of vocabulary to the student (S):

(T): *This is a pen.* Then the teacher should make beckoning motions to 'invite' the student to repeat the phrase.

(S): *This is a pen.* Then the teacher must nod, smile, and enthuse over the correct repetition made by the student.

(T): *Is it a rubber?* The teacher asks this question whilst shaking his head and mouthing the word 'No'.

(S): *No.*

(T): *Very good.* Again, the teacher smiles and exudes admiration for the clever student who has just given the correct reply.

(T): *Is it a lamp?*

(S): *No.*

(T): *Very good... Is it a pen?* This the teacher asks while waving the pen under the nose of the student, mouthing the answer 'Yes', and nodding profusely.

(S): *Yes.*

(I): *Very good.* The next stage for the teacher is to ask 'either/or' questions. Here, the 'Beesleys Method' instructs the teacher to give the correct reply as the second part of the question.

(I): *Is it an elephant or a pen?* The teacher should constantly gesticulate: shaking his head whilst mouthing the word 'elephant', and nod enthusiastically when saying 'pen'.

(S): *It is a pen.*

(I): *Yes, very good.*

(I): *Is it a cup of coffee or a pen?*

(S): *It is a pen.*

(I): *Very good.* The next step is to ask questions without the answer – in this case 'pen' – being in the questions themselves…

(I): *What is it?*

(S): *It is a pen.*

(I): *Very good.*

(I): *What is it?*

(S): *It is a rubber.*

(I): *Very good.*

(I): *What is it?*

(S): *It is a cup.*

(I): *Very good.*

(I): *What is it?*

(S): *It is a pen.*

(I): *Very good.* The final stage is whereby the teacher mixes up the three forms of questions while making confidence-building purring sounds and waving about enthusiastically.

(I): *Is it a rubber?*

(S): *No.*

(I): *Is it a cup or a pen?*

(S): *It is a pen.*

(I): *Very good.*

(T): *Is it a chair?*

(S): *No.*

(T): *Is it a pen?*

(S): *Yes.*

(T): *What is it?*

(S): *It is a pen?*

(T): *Yes, very good.*

The teacher is not really a teacher in the true sense of the word at all. When the Beesleys teachers' book, which every teacher in every Beesleys centre must religiously follow, says it is time to teach the word 'pen', the word 'pen' must be taught. The teacher has no input whatsoever when it comes to the contents of his class. The teacher simply reads out what is in the teachers' book; and maybe asks 'Is it an elephant or a pen?' Instead of 'Is it a book or a pen?'

So, why then, knowing all this, did I even bother climbing those stairs with the burger bar colours? Well, because they were there. And I needed a job. Once I was working somewhere and had a little security and reassurance that I would be able to stay in Berlin, I would look for something better. My priority was to live in Berlin for a substantial amount of time. And whether or not this wish would be realised depended upon my ability to find employment before my savings ran out.

I explained to the receptionist why I was there and enquired as to whether it would be possible to talk to the Director of the school about obtaining a teaching post. The receptionist had bright red lipstick on, a thick layer of foundation, and too many teeth in her head. She looked like an airhostess. She talked to her boss via the intercom and then showed me through to the Director's office. I greeted the Director, a power-dressing woman *extraordinaire*, and offered her my hand. She shook it and indicated for me to be seated. She was in her late thirties, and had been for quite some time. She had an American slur that had probably been perfected after many years of having waffles for breakfast.

Her bureau was full of office toys, locked glass cabinets, unused fountain pens, and feng shui. It was a CJ office, and I hoped my chair made a farting noise as I sat down. It did not... I explained my situation and my qualifications, and handed her my photocopies. She took them from me and placed them on the desk in front of her without even glancing at them.

She had an expensive hair cut, a bit Mary Quant and a bit basin bowl; and a fake tan that if she did not lay off the sun bed and the carotene for a while, I thought, would end up making her look the shade of one of those 40 feet killer Amazonian women from one of those fifties 'B' movies.

She was petite with chunky-heeled black boots, black tights, and a black pencil midi-skirt. Her eyebrows were pencilled in, as was her smile. Her conversation was unfalteringly professional and gave nothing away of herself. She sat in her padded swivel black leather armchair, and swivelled. She had a long grey jacket on, which reached down to her thighs. She talked and talked about Beesleys and its ethics, its approach to language learning, its founder and its history – and on and on she went. And I did not care, but I smiled in the right places and looked interested in all the other places. Eventually she came down to the nitty gritty. She told me that although no new teachers were required in any of their three Berlin centres, the Head of their Leipzig centre who had recently contacted her would be requiring staff in five weeks time. And she enquired as to whether I would be interested in such a posting. I did not think about it too much at the time, and simply said yes.

I walked outside to a rainbow and puddles on the pavement. I went to Checkpoint Charlie and crossed from former West to former East. I got myself some noodles and mixed vegetables in one of the many roadside cabins. I took a long walk to Prenzlauer Berg under the ribbed Berlin skies. I ambled into a bar called Celtic Fusion, ordered a pint and began talking to the Irish barman.

After two pints, I left. And headed for the address that the barman had written onto the back of a beer-mat for me. It was where a friend of his lived, who was moving back to Britain in two days time.

I slept on the settee for the two days that Eddie, that was the guy's name, remained in the flat. He showed me how to get the antiquated coal-burning oven started. He gave me the address of where to send my rent to. And then at about 11.30 in the evening of his last day, he left.

A couple of days after settling in, I decided to have a wander around to get accustomed to my new locale. Then… um, that's it… about three weeks later, in ample time to find accommodation, I headed for Leipzig and, at least I believed at the time, employment.

XIII

Most of my time in Berlin escapes me now. An occasional recollection drifts this way and that – and I'm certain some of it happened. Maybe all of it did... It is sometimes difficult to distinguish fact from fiction. But isn't that always the way?

I vaguely remember finding a doctor's surgery in Linien Straße. Linien Straße was just round the corner from Oranienburger Straße; on which was a crumbling squatted artists' commune called *Tacheles*. It was all post-apocalyptic with twisted welded metal everywhere. And it was in this bar that I waited before heading for my appointment to see the doctor. I bought a half-litre glass of beer and went to sit at a rusting metal sculpted table. An aging drunk punk came to talk to me. All I remember of the conversation is that he told me that in the seventies he and his girlfriend were on holiday in Port Lligat in northern Spain, which was the village where Salvador Dali lived.

The punk and his girlfriend had been wandering around on the rocks that looked over the little port there. Some of the rocks on that gnarled landscape Dali would paint and include them in his canvases, often with contorted timepieces hanging from their weather-beaten surfaces. The punk told me that Dali appeared from... [*No, the preposition 'from' isn't required. It is more satisfactory for the mind to leave Dali's arrival as ethereal. For this is how my mind was beginning to operate at this time... and certainly how it is operating now.*]

...Dali *appeared* to the couple, and he invited them back to his house. They were plied with drinks and shown around the dwelling, which was the 'Dalian' mind as represented in bricks and mortar: portals, labyrinthine passageways, distorting mirrors, Greek sculptures wearing gas masks, kitsch advertising hoardings, giant red eggs, and a beautiful view of the bay – it was an egotistical place, self-aggrandising, and self-doubting... As is every mind, I suppose.

The couple were then shown into the circular room with its North African semi-circular settees. They were given more drinks before Dali offered them a substantial amount of money to have sex in front of him... They declined the offer, according to the punk. And shortly afterwards made their excuses and left.

The strange thing was that the punk's girlfriend was called Caroline. And as he told me this he gave me a wink. And... well... or, at least that's what my memory tells me happened. But despite the episode with my 'own' Caroline still perturbing the recesses of my conscience, I was sure that the punk's Caroline was not my Caroline. No no, it couldn't have been – the age would have been all wrong...

Just a coincidence then – that's it, just a coincidence. But I do recall that at this time I had the feeling things were 'completing' – somewhat as if two points of a circle were close to joining. And I remember that the words 'hole' and 'whole' were preoccupying me... but possibly this was no more than a game I was playing with myself. But is there not something very satisfying about two words that sound the same, and yet have different meanings – different meanings that can nevertheless be extended to mean the same thing?

I'd decided to visit the doctor because I hadn't felt too good for a while. For two days prior to seeing the doctor I'd been coughing up blood, and I cannot remember for how long before that – since it had been so sporadic – I'd been having cramps. I suppose 'cramps' is the correct word; sometimes I would have sharp prolonged internal pains for no reason I could identify. And then they'd disappear, sometimes for ages – and I'd forget all about them... But I didn't believe it was related to my state of mind.

He was a strange little man with staring eyes and a waxen moustache. He wasn't wearing a monocle, but he did have a red circle around his left eye. As if he had been peering through one of those joke telescopes you could buy from newsagents years ago. But I seem to recall that they left black marks around the eye, not red. Whatever the cause of this disfiguration, I quickly dispelled the thought.

He told me that I needed some tests. He took a couple of phials of blood, and asked me to go behind the screen to urinate into a small plastic bottle, which I did… He then instructed me to return in three days time for the results. But I'm pretty certain I never did…

What I am as sure as sure can be about is that when my time had come – or rather when it was time for me to move on – I took the U-bahn to the Central Station and caught the next train to Leipzig. The German trains, although modern, had maintained some of the old-style compartments with the sliding doors for just eight people to sit in.

I pulled the sliding door behind me and sat in the empty compartment. There was a torn and dishevelled looking newspaper on the seat next to me… I turned from the newspaper to the view out of the window. I watched tired and transfixed as the skyline of Berlin soon transformed into the rose-flamed twilight skies of the former East Germany. The trees and clouds passed by my window at differing paces. And I felt dozy.

I placed the newspaper on the seat facing me so I could put my feet up without making a mark on the rusty orange coloured upholstery. As I'd picked it up and folded it to form a rectangle to put my feet on, I noticed an envelope that had been on the seat underneath it. I picked it up. It was wrinkly, evidently from having been wet at some stage. It was dry now but the writing was smudged to such an extent as to make the recipient's name and address illegible. The top right hand corner of the envelope where the stamp had been was missing, torn off. Yet the first two letters of the postmark had been missed and remained decipherable: 'Ox'… Oxford? Oxbow, Canada? …Oxford?

It had been jaggedly opened by someone in a rush, is what I thought as I slipped the contents out and began to read it:

Many many distances away Shöana walked across a beach barefoot – listening to the sound of the gulls and the sea lapping at the sun-cooked sand. With the spring in her step and the slight breeze coming off the ocean, her black hair was delicately bouncing up and down on her shoulders and back. Her green eyes matched the colour of the sea, as did the single strand of green beads threaded into her hair. Her light sky blue dress – light both in terms of colour and weight – flowed rhythmically along with her hair. Her skin was the shade of a well-baked biscuit, and her lips suggested the hint of a smile. She held her sandals and Camus' *The Outsider* in her right hand, in her left was a clay pipe from which she would occasionally inhale.

She paused for a moment to gaze out to the sea and sky that bled into each other on the unreachable horizon. With a slight flick of the head she deflected the few strands of hair that had gathered in front of her eyes, and turned to consider the footsteps she had left on this desolate sandscape. She sat down and faced the water, and she peered and wondered what would become of her. And as she did so she distractedly scooped away divots of sand with her clenched toes, making little holes that she could quarry her feet into.

The sea lapped at the beach, the sun bleached down onto the sand, and Shöana basked in the warm glow that surrounded her. She twisted her torso and plumped up a little mound of sand behind her. She placed her hands either side of her, lifted her bottom off the ground, and propelled herself forwards. She lowered her bottom at the spot where she believed she would be at the right distance to enable her to lean backwards until her head lowered directly onto her cushion made of sand. And then to sleep, and to dream… to dream about the one hundred and sixty-seven moons, and to memorise the difference between the cold and life-giving warmth…

Physical beauty was one thing, but this type of beauty was the much more valuable purity of thought; and this particular purity of thought was indivisible ( ). Shöana was pure in thought and pure in deed, and nothing was more beautiful than that… Shöana was a realist – she always reached for the impossible.

If everything that was about to happen was justice, if this was what she deserved, the balance had tipped too far... And at that precise moment, a long long way away, geographically, lovers walked barefoot in the rubble, watched over by faceless snipers.

Shöana lazily opened one eye shortly followed by the other. Something had summoned her back from her whirlpool dream world. She squinted out over the sea in the direction of the yellow summer sun. Then almost reluctantly – as if she knew she was on the brink of something that was going to shatter her tranquillity – she turned her head to the left, along the beach, but there was nothing of note. Slowly she turned back to face the direction she'd come from, and there in the distance was a man-shape... a man-shape accompanied by a dog-shape.

Shöana rose to her haunches, and as she did so the keeper released the dog from his leash. The dog careered along the beach in Shöana's direction like a greyhound from a trap – he wasn't a greyhound though. And within the time it takes for the mind and body to reach a state of panic Shöana's eyes had darted between the large brute heading in her direction and the forest. And she'd calculated whether she'd make it to the trees before the dog made it to her – it was going to be a close thing.

Shöana ran like a sprinter on drugs. She reached the trees terrified and out of breath. *Running forever running,* was the thought that passed through her dislocated mind. She grimaced as the intense pain of running over broken branches and undergrowth without her sandals, hit her brain. She ran and ran; her heart pumped, her breath raced, and her dress ripped.

Why she was on the run Shöana was not sure. Could it really simply be down to the fact that she was who she was, she did what she did, she did not infringe on anyone else's space, she respected others as she respected herself, and she was quite happy thank you very much? Surely not.

She tripped over a tree stump; as she instinctively attempted to break her fall she gashed her left hand on a broken soft drinks bottle... As she heaved herself up, ensuring that most of her weight was on her right hand, she heard a snarl from behind her. She edged herself around on all fours. The vicious looking beast, fully pointed, stood watching her. Slowly, very slowly, Shöana held out her hand in a gesture of friendship. The dog snarled, saliva dripping from its mouth. Shöana snapped her hand away.

After gathering herself, she tentatively tried again to make a friend of this creature, with a mind to making a dash for it. Shöana stared fondly into the brute's eyes whilst speaking in lullaby tones, and once again very cautiously she offered her hand in peace. The dog snarled. Palm up, she continued to offer her hand in a gesture of friendship. An offering; an offering of herself – of the person she was. She was showing that she posed no threat, she meant no harm, and had no malice.

The dog although perpetuating its rumbling growl from the deep cavernous inners of its throat began nevertheless half-heartedly to sniff Shöana's hand. This was at least slight progress, but even while inhaling Shöana's scent it did not once take its eyes off her… Trying to gain its confidence was a laborious task, and time was running out.

Her heart hung heavily in her ribcage. Desperate sadness washed through her. Once again she found herself in a position over which she had no control… She did not deserve this; she did not deserve anyone thinking that she deserved this. There were things out there that were greater than her. She had known that before, but she had almost allowed herself to forget. She had allowed her defences to lower; she had allowed herself the rare luxury of letting her guard down.

Who were these people who were controlling, distorting, and preventing the empowerment of the spirit? She felt as though a mirror had been put up around the world to stop people looking any further. People had wilfully climbed into shatterproof glass. Who were these bastards who knew best – and yet did not?

Just then the uniformed number stole into view. With hunger in his squinted eyes, promotion in his head, and malice on his lips – he gave a command and the dog heeled.

The guard towered over Shöana's outstretched trembling body and shouted: "You've pushed us too far for too long, this isn't the way things work. Stop pushing against the wall. It ain't the way things work. Just think what a terrible mess we'd be in if everyone was like that. You're just gonna have to cut it out… or rather *we're* going to have to cut it out for you." Shöana could smell his rotten breath. "There are rules, right... and rules have to be obeyed, right. There are those who make the rules, and then there are the rest of us, right, who have to follow the rules," he spat. "There has to be some order, some structure. I mean, just think about it, right – otherwise there'd just be chaos. We have to accept the unarguable wisdom of those above us, otherwise why would they be above us... Of course, sometimes what they say, or tell us to do, may seem odd, but they do have a good reason for everything they do. Even if it seems strange at the time, we have to trust them."

Shöana wanted to cry but wouldn't allow herself. "Right then," he continued, "shortly I will take you back to the compound for 're-aligning', but," he paused to smile, "we have a little time yet." And with that his smile broadened to reveal his two front blackening teeth, as he began to undo his belt.

"You'll enjoy this," he dribbled. "It'll be good practice for you to stop making a fuss and start accepting what your superiors want." He undid the top button on his nicely creased trousers. Shöana began pleading with him, but as she did so the dog advanced a little closer, making a throaty growl...

Shöana was struggling and kicking in a world, and against a world, which she had no control over. And she was falling, spiralling downwards from a cliff made from other people's intrusions and institutions. Cliffs and tumbling precipices made from their ice-cold ways of thinking, as they persisted in constructing their towers and dungeons in the snow.

The man in white satin on the not too distant plateau-horizon watched over, sad and disgusted in his solemnity. His stare was directed towards Shöana – with amber eyes, with an amber-eyed beam shinning down. And then, slowly, weightlessly, she felt herself rising... She rose with an incredible lightness of being, and she realised that a feeling of easiness and tranquillity had engulfed her. And she was no longer panicked by the events in which she had been the principal character.

Feeling confident and new, she stood up and through the scene that had been playing, turning round and around within the amber hue that was engulfing her. And she floated gently upwards and looked down over where she had been lying. She saw herself and him motionless, caught in suspended animation: a still from a film that should never be shot; an image of horror caught in the act, and stopped and silenced until a moment when it could be edited, cut-out, or rewound forever.

Shöana continued floating along in the breeze, immersed in her shimmering yellow-orange glow; until she was gently lowered onto the edge of the plateau where the man dressed all in white had stood... But now was gone.

I put the words in my pocket, and wondered what it all meant... Was it somebody's forgotten letter? An incomplete story? An experience, possibly? Or, an opinion? It all seems so strange now – almost as if it never happened...

My gaze and my thoughts reverted to the dusk-light through my window. My eyes made patterns in the sky, with the help of the clouds and the dying sun. And I knew that when they appeared, if I thought I was able, I would count the stars.

------•••------

And I'm tired and I can feel a coldness clawing me into its claustrophobic embrace. And I feel like a cross between a character in one of Goya's paintings and a Henry Moore sculpture: happy and sad, smooth and grotesque.

------•••------

The train continued trundling along in its southerly direction. The last trace of the day's light was curling up behind the clouds. The wafer-thin brittle burnt darkness of night would shortly be all that remained of the day. The lights from my urgent locomotive lit up the bushes and trees along the verge. But it was an unsatisfying light; a light that gave you no time to focus, severed as it was by thick dark strips where the carriages joined each other.

I wondered what would greet my time in Leipzig. I was on the brink of my future, and I was prepared to dive straight in. I thought about the flat where I would live and the friends that I was going to meet. It was all there waiting for me – as soon as I got off the train, it would begin. The apartment in which I was going to reside awaited my arrival, and I wondered what it looked like. And now that all of this is coming back to me, I vaguely recall enjoying a prolonged consideration of the whole new chapter of adventures that I believed were about to unfold. All the people that I would soon meet – some of them lovers, some of them colleagues, some just people I would have brief conversations with whilst having a coffee somewhere – they were all there.

Unbeknownst to any of them I was about to change their lives, as they were about to change mine. Maybe not in a momentous way, but *change* was coming all the same. Possibly, I would get married and have children there, I doubted it, but it was possible. Everyone that I was going to meet and everything I was going to do was already there for me, awaiting my arrival...

XIV

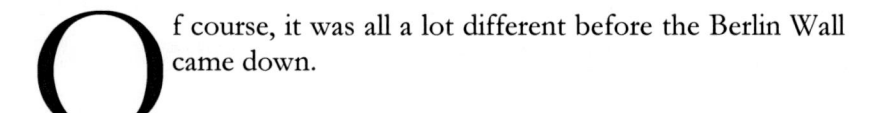

Of course, it was all a lot different before the Berlin Wall came down.

•

It escapes me now as to the reason why I never turned up for the training course, which could have resulted in my gaining employment as a teacher. Nor can I recall where I stayed during those first nights in Leipzig. Nor, now I come to think of it, can I recall where I stayed during those first few weeks in that new town.

Amongst the haze of new faces, trams, bars, and buildings, I remember quite vividly a shop. Though to call it simply a 'shop' in no way accurately portrays its true essence, and promotes the status and experience of shops to a hitherto unimaginable level… It was a womb and an organism that had little connection with the outside world.

It was a warehouse, or a former factory, that could only be reached along a narrow winding alleyway; an alleyway that curled itself between tall windowless buildings. It would only have been possible for two people to pass each other if one of them turned sideways. Not that I ever remember having seen one other soul coming to or going from the shop.

The entrance of the alleyway was between two crumbling derelict buildings half way along a nondescript back street. Overhead a pipe leaked its cracked water. Often a puddle had to be sidestepped or leaped before one's first proper stride could be made into the alleyway. Even on a hot sunny day the air in the alleyway always seemed cold and stagnant. It was possible that when the sun was directly overhead the warm rays streamed in – but I never saw it.

No sign announced and no placard proclaimed – either that it was *the* shop or that it was *a* shop.

Once through the large windowless double doors, you were confronted by a vastness that teetered full of a seemingly endless array of disparate objects. There were no neat lanes or rows, only meandering pathways that wove between the stacked-high shelves. Shelves that were piled high with books, papers, ashtrays, mugs, signs, containers, helmets, and many other things (some of which I had no idea what they were for) all mixed together randomly on top of each other.

Intermittently there was a break between the shelves. Three angled sofas, a coffee table, an ashtray, and an old coffee vending machine, had been placed together to create a 'relaxation point'. A place where the weary traveller – no, I mean 'shopper'… where the weary shopper could sit down for a few minutes to contemplate his next move.

Behind the counter, which was an antiquated writing desk, was a sign attached to the wall. It was written in four languages: Russian, German, French, and English. The English read: 'You Are Leaving The American Sector'.

The proprietor, if that is what he was – although, I seem to remember that I grew to see him more like a curator to this strange land – was in his late-fifties. He wore an apron, one of those brown leather aprons that carpenters or shoemakers wear. His moustache was of the handlebar variety. And he wore a pair of precariously balanced pince-nez spectacles on the end of his reddened pockmarked nose.

On the rare occasions that he looked up from whatever it was that he was doing – reading a book or tinkering with the inners of a radio – he would acknowledge my presence with a slight nod and a lip-clenched smile.

And despite his tendency to be curt, I liked him. And I remember that the more I considered his comments, the more I realised that he was not being rude at all, it was merely his way of imparting information that in his opinion I should have known.

One time I wanted to purchase something that had caught my eye, although what it was escapes me now. I made my way to the counter. And this was quite a feat in itself, since 'the shop' was so vast; and it was also impossible to see over from one aisle to another, because the shelves and crates were so highly stacked. You couldn't even see very far along the aisle you were in, since not one of the aisles I had seen was straight.

On eventually finding my way to the counter, I held the item out in front of me and produced some Deutsch Marks, which I placed on the counter for the inattentive proprietor to take the required amount. He raised his eyes from the mechanism he was toying with to inform me that if I wished to spend my *West* German money I should go to an Intershop[1].

Intershops were the shops in East German times where tourists could go to spend their foreign currency; not only tourists but also citizens who happened to have foreign currency. The shops sold goods from the West, which you could not get hold of in the normal East German shops. I had known none of this at the time. And instead of questioning what the proprietor meant, I stood rooted to my spot for several seconds contemplating what to do next.

With my un-purchased item still in my hand, and the proprietor tinkering away once again, I quietly sidled off in the direction I had come. My initial thoughts of returning the item to where I had found it were soon abandoned however. For, as I looked at the enormity of it all I realised how impossible it would be to retrace my steps amongst the multitude of similar looking pathways. So, as I walked away from the counter and the proprietor, I popped the item onto a shelf at random. And I remember thinking that it looked as though it belonged in the place

I'd chosen for it. But I could probably have placed it anywhere and it would have fitted in, melting into the totality as unobtrusively as if it had always been there.

I wandered and thought, picked things up, examined them, and put them down again. The place smelt of yesterday – even though I did not know what yesterday had smelt like. I turned a corner and came upon one of the comfortable relaxation points. It consisted of three sofas at right angles to each other: one orange, one blue, and one brown; fraying, patched, and threadbare to differing degrees.

Next to the brown sofa was a red plastic armless seventies style swivel office chair. On its grey metal foot was a label that read 'Karl Marx Universität Leipzig'. Behind the orange sofa was a drinks machine. I took a 1 Deutsch Mark coin out of my pocket, reached over, and tried to put it into the slot, but it didn't fit.

On the coffee table was a pile of coins. I looked at them and then at the 1 Deutsch Mark in my hand, and then back to the pile of ten or twelve coins. I picked the coins up with my right hand. The coins were light in weight and felt like toy money. On closer examination I saw that they were East German Marks. And then somewhat flummoxed, I looked from the 1 Ost Mark piece I'd separated from the others, to the West German Deutsch Mark I'd placed on the table. And I spent a moment wondering what a pile of East German coins was doing there.

I took the coin with a 1 on it and placed it into the slot. It fitted perfectly. I pressed the button marked Moccamix[2]. And once the liquid had drizzled its way into the cup, I sat down on the orange sofa with my coffee-like drink in hand. I took a sip and then gazed at the lopsided shelving across the aisle from me. Then I peered along the aisle to my right, and then to my left. Books were piled upon books; a Zenit[3] camera was next to a bust of Lenin; a large round clock with no hands sat propped up against a book entitled Sozialismus deine Welt[4] – the book that every East German school child received in their fourteenth year. And I spotted a cigarette packet with the word Sprachlos[5] boldly emblazoned across its front, next to which was a pile of sports medals from Spartakiade[6] – the Communist Olympics.

Things appeared to have been placed where they were without any interpretable reason or pattern. It was disorder on a colossal scale. But every so often I came across a break in the shelves where there was a 'show' kitchen. Admittedly, a very old fashioned 'show' kitchen, but a very clean and tidy fully functioning kitchen none the less. These kitchens all had walls on three sides and no ceiling; the drawers had cutlery in them, and there was always a fully stocked fridge…

I took a sip of my drink and placed it on the table. I put the remaining coins back into a neat pile next to the ashtray. The ashtray was an old bar ashtray, with the logo for some beer called Hell[7] printed on it. There was a solitary butt in the ashtray. I picked it up. It had lipstick on it. It was a peculiar shade of lipstick, a sort of silvery turquoise. And as I glared down at its shade a small jolt from some long forgotten memory rippled through me, not enough of a jolt to give me any satisfactory recollection of anything. But it was a shudder of having seen something similar somewhere else.

The only way I can really describe the 'jolt' I received from seeing the lipstick-stained filter is that it was similar to a *déjà vu* flash. It left me with slight uneasy after-tones. And the other odd thing about the filter was that it was warm to the touch. And that meant that the filter was the only object I had come across whilst in the shop that was of 'now'.

I took out my rolling tobacco from my pocket and began to roll a cigarette. I placed the cigarette paper on the coffee table. Then I sprinkled tobacco along three-quarters of its length. And in the remaining space I fastidiously, almost ceremonially, placed the lipstick-sodden butt. I then bound it tight, with the precision and obsessive care given to a geisha girl's foot. For some inexplicable reason I wanted to own it, to possess it, to breath it in. The soiled filter was a part of something or a link to something that I felt could help me…

I took another drink of my coffee and lit my cigarette. It tasted strange – but that was possibly because I was not used to filter-tipped cigarettes… Shortly afterwards I fell asleep. It was a deep sleep, yet an uneasy one. I dreamt of a woman leaving me. I never saw her face, or if I did, I did not remember it when I awoke.

I think she was waving to me – waving goodbye to me. I remember her departure made me feel both happy and sad; but why I felt either of these emotions was unclear. She may have been holding a cigarette in her hand as she left. Or maybe that was just me projecting my waking thoughts onto my dream-world...

The clock with no hands on one of the shelves to my right gave me no clue as to how long I had been asleep (although, as the Swedish say, even a clock that is broken is correct twice a day). The coffee cup was as I had left it: two-thirds full. The dark brown gooey liquid was stone cold. My rolling tobacco was on the table, next to which was a single cigarette paper three-quarters full of tobacco. There was no sign of the woman's filter. I looked under the coffee table in case it had been knocked onto the floor. But there was nothing there except for a piece of paper. And there was nothing in the ashtray either, except for ash (probably the amount of ash that a single cigarette would create).

I put some more tobacco in the cigarette and finished rolling. I felt groggy. I was certain I had at least started smoking my rollie before nodding off; but I shrugged the thought off, dwelling upon such things wouldn't get me anywhere... I sat back and inhaled, and watched the yellowy-blue smoke curling crazy patterns up to the sky (ceiling).

It was then I noticed that the small pile of seven or eight coins had greatly increased. The seven or eight coins had transformed into about twenty coins and five notes... I balanced my roll-up on one of the inverted nipples of the astray and counted the East German money. Then I got out my wallet in order to count out the equivalent West German tender, deciding that I had no use for it in this place. Irritatingly I didn't quite have the matching amount. But I figured that it didn't really matter and put all my West German currency on the coffee table and pocketed the Ost Marks[8]... Now, if I saw anything that took my fancy I would be able to purchase it from the proprietor without any of his cryptic comments.

I picked up my cigarette again and relit it. And I felt contented with what I had done... With a pocket full of legal tender (legal, at least in this place) I felt less of an outsider; I strangely felt more a part of the shop. I had become, at least in my mind, less of a customer – although ultimately I suppose that is what I was – and more of, well, an *exhibit*. Yes, an exhibit: I was more a part of the whole fabric of 'the shop'.

For, as time unceasingly progressed I realised that this was a museum as much as it was a shop (although museum was not quite the word I was looking for). I remained unclear, however, as to whether this was the unfiltered truth or merely my perception of how things were. But either way, or whatever the cause was, I felt I belonged. And an easy feeling of wellbeing permeated my self. And possibly this was the first time I had felt such a lightness of being in a long while. Inexplicably, it was a sensation that told me – at this particular juncture, and given the journey I had travelled – there was no more appropriate place for me to be…

I picked up the piece of paper that lay under the coffee table. It was a list of the 'Presidents' of the DDR. It read: Wilhelm Pieck (1949-1960); Walter Ulbricht (1960-1973); Willi Stoph (1973-1976); Erich Honecker (1976-1989); Egon Krenz (1989-1989); Hans Modrow and Manfred Gerlach (1989-1990); Lothar de Maiziere and Sabine Bergmann (1990-1990)[9].

I placed the paper on the table, took a swig of my cold coffee-like drink, and stood and stretched. It was time to move on. It looked as if I was only about a quarter of the way in and to my recollection I hadn't ventured any deeper towards the centre of this maze yet. I say to my 'recollection' because my sleep – if that's what it was – had slightly disorientated me.

I headed in the direction I believed would take me to the unknown depths of 'the shop'. I walked round a corner and then another and another. I came to a crossing of the ways but opted to continue along the path I was on, which I sensed was taking me towards the middle.

There was dullish grey light everywhere – artificial and electric, but too much was going on at eye level to look up and see where it originated from… I picked up a plastic object from a shelf. It was flat, but you could concertina it up so that it made a cup; on its bottom was a mirror. I liked it. I guessed it was for camping – easily packed away. I decided to have it, for novelty value if nothing else. And I put it in my pocket with the intention of purchasing it on my way out. I was sure that I had enough money to buy it since it was only a small thing; but with no prices on anything it was difficult to tell.

I looked in the mirror – dusty rusty mirror. I had the beginnings of a beard. I did not think I had had a beard before. No, I'm sure I had not had a beard before. Then again, sometimes I was too lazy to shave. And with this in mind, I wondered when the last time I had shaved was.

Albeit that I could picture myself with a razor in my hand I could not recollect where the image was from: a chrome-shiny bathroom with its spotless mirrors. I felt slightly perturbed at not recalling where these fractured memories came from. And noticing that I looked dark under the eyes I put the mirror-cup in my pocket and rubbed my face with my grimy hands. And my scratchy, wiry face made me think about *time*, time and the history of time – but only briefly.

A thought, undefined, and yet blinding and sharp like a streak of lightning, propelled me down an avenue of uncontrolled and uncontrollable behaviour – like a twilight tourette's sufferer with a singular twitch, I rubbed my face. And I kept rubbing it, harder and harder. It itched, and it was unclean. And I continued to rub it with the palms of my hands. Up and down, up and down – and in circular motions like one does when washing ones face. The circular motions of my hands increased in pressure, harder and harder – pressing harder and harder.

I closed my eyes and started swaying to the pressure I was exerting on myself. It was a primal sway to the body's internal rhythms, to the electrical currents and the pumping of the blood. I fell to my knees, onto the dusty epoch-stained carpet. I knelt in a worshipping position, my head facing upwards towards a non-existent sun. I believe I passed out, or maybe my consciousness was elsewhere…

------•••------

Words are both a facilitator and a hindrance.

------•••------

I was lying on a floor, a floor of a bathroom. A bathroom that was full of steam and shiny metal. The tiles appeared to be seeping blood around my head. Their coldness soothed my throbbing temples… She stood above me, naked, one leg either side of my torso. She was bending down, squatting over me with a razor in her hand. The strokes she made against my skin were deft, delicate movements that did not distract me from my other contemplations. I could not see her face, yet I knew who she was. Or, I had known who she was, once. And, like bathing in warm ass' milk, I felt sexy and innocent and easily succumbed to whatever it was I had been summoned there to succumb to.

And this was real and should have been disturbing; yet, all the other dreams had been real too.

I came to lying on my side in one of the aisles of the shop. I scratched my head and felt relief to see the strip-lighting above my head. I stared up at the distant ceiling and distractedly reached into my trouser pocket for my mirror-cup. I held the mirror above my face and noticed blood on my left hand. After wiping it on my trousers, I saw that the abrasion was in the middle of my palm. It was nothing I chose to focus my attention upon however, and discarded it as meaningless.

The mirror told me that I needed a shave and to brush my hair. I raised myself onto all fours first, looked around like an inquisitive hound, and then I pushed myself upright. I walked and wondered who the woman had been. And as I considered whether she really was familiar to me or just seemed familiar whilst dreaming, I came across a large wooden chest. It reminded me of a treasure chest, with rusty locks and bolts attached to its side. On the top of the chest was an electric razor. It had AKA[11] written on its side, which I presumed was the make. I put it in my inside jacket pocket professing to pay for it, along with the mirror-cup, on my way out.

The pathway looped around a swirling corner till eventually I was heading back towards what, with my dislodged sense of direction, I still perceived to be the middle of this labyrinth. As I turned the final section of the bend, a cream-coloured cabin came into view. On its door was written *Páni* and *Dámi*. Later I discovered the words meant 'Men' and 'Women' in Czech.

I climbed the three metal steps. I stood on the top step and peered inside. The cabin was full of basins, urinals, and mirrors. The mirrors were spotlessly clean, and the lighting had a hair-salon luminosity to it, which made me look good. I gazed for far too long at my reflections in the circus of mirrors. I looked interesting and blemish-free; and nothing like how I felt, nor how my pocket mirror-cup had portrayed its version of the truth to me. Nevertheless, I went with it and enjoyed looking at myself while I plugged my shaver in and began shaving. After several minutes of the stuttered electric purring sound, I splashed my face with the ice-cold water. Its temperature made me gasp at first, and then it gave me a refreshing zing that set me on my way.

The next bend in the aisle was a double-bend: first to the right, then to the left. But I decided it was probably better to think of it as a wave than a double-bend. A little further along the carpeting was replaced by linoleum, black linoleum with markings on it: white oblong dotted lines, like the surface of a road, were down its middle. And as the carpet turned into linoleum so the contents of the shelves altered, as did the entire atmosphere of the place...

Difficult though it was at first to identify what the more subtle changes were in this new part of the shop, I settled upon the conclusion that each person's experience within the shop would not be identical. A person would perceive the shop-space according to his preconceived ideas; preconceived ideas based upon what he had been told the truth was most likely to be.

Then, for a moment, I stopped and gazed motionless at the shelves to my left, and I wondered if my realisation was truth or subjective spirals of over analysis. And I began to feel as though I were also a product on a rickety shelf. And where I ended up and settled in this great vastness would decide my fate and ascertain whether I would become one type of product over another.

Would I end up being a rubberstamp on a dusty export form, a utilitarian product that has a retrospective quirky appeal to it, a readymade, or something throw-away? A chocolate rush or a paper plane, long term, or a flash in the pan of fools' gold? And I knew that where I was heading, and where I decided to plant my flag, would determine the future – my future… But either way, I refused to be an aid to product placement research. Not after all that could have been; not after knowing that everything had only ever been just slightly out of reach.

I spied a bike bell, a car lamp, and an un-completed form for the only motoring insurance company in East German times. I passed a number plate, a motor-bike helmet, a Stern[12] mono radio-tape player, and a pile of old tram tickets – the ones for adults had *20 Pfennig* printed on them, and the children's had *10 Pfennig* on them – all lay circled around a wing mirror on an upturned wooden crate.

After several minutes, I shook myself out of my stasis and moved on. I came to a T-junction that was laid out like a miniature meeting of roads. The road signs were scaled down versions of the real thing. I turned right, then after only five strides the linoleum lane turned 90° to the left and opened up onto a parking place, where sixteen cars were parked in a grid of four by four. I stood there for what seemed like ages. And I stared at this bizarre metal square, which to my mind had materialised the same way as a spaceship might.

To the right of the opening was a table. On the table was a booklet with a picture of an automobile on its cover. I took it from the table, and on seeing a white East German lawn chair I went and sat down. I looked across the space at all the unfamiliar cars for a few moments, and then I opened the booklet and began to read. The booklet was full of pictures of cars and text in both German and English. The text gave a description of each of the cars parked in front of me coupled with a history of the East German car industry.

I spent a little over ten minutes sitting there looking at the pictures in the booklet and reading snippets of the text. But then I got bored and wanted to take a closer look at these cars that had no place to go, no owner, and no way of getting home. Their time had gone, but possibly the twists of yesterday could have thrown up something different, something to be proud of... Maybe they did...

The four DDR cars were situated nearest to me, end to end making up the first column: *Wartburg*; *Wartburg Melkus* – which was a kit car; *Krause-Duo* – which was a car for disabled people; and a *Trabant* – which was painted a colour known as 'Trabbie Green'... I made my way along this outer column and peered in the windows to see how their interiors compared to... compared to... oh... compared to something or other.

The second row consisted of cars uniquely from the USSR. I made my way from one to the next. From the *Lada* and *Moscvitz*, to the *Saporosh* and *Wolga*. The first car in the next row, a black painted *Shiguli*, also originated from the Soviet Union. However, the subsequent three cars, all painted in differing shades of off white, came from Czechoslovakia, Poland, and Rumania respectively: *Skoda*, *Polska Fiat*; and *Dacia*.

The fourth and final row was the most interesting of all. It contained four cars that were only sporadically accessible to East German citizens. The availability of the Yugoslavian *Zastava*, for example, depended upon the state of DDR/Yugoslavian relations; and, the Swedish *Volvo*, West German *VW Golf*, and, the Japanese *Mazda 323*, were only ever occasionally available – imported as they were in batches of 10,000[13]...

This parking place was the most uncluttered area that I had come across in the shop. Hanging from the ceiling on all four sides of this parking lot were thick grey curtains that overlapped each other, made from something that resembled coal sack material. The word 'funnel' dovetailed into my thoughts. I was inside a massive industrial chimney – the cars were the fuel and the spotlights were the flames. And I was the fire starter... crazy fire starter.

I moved on and out of there... And it was only a couple of bends away from where the cars were parked that I came across another of the relaxation points. I was weary, and after rummaging around for several minutes I found a rolled up sleeping bag on a nearby shelf. I lay down on the middle of the three settees, and with relief, like a giant green worm, I slipped inside the sleeping bag and covered my face. I slept like an all-night parking lot attendant from the seedier end of town: fitfully, and with one ear constantly on guard.

When I was awake I fuelled my thoughts with rollie cigarettes and East German coffee from the machine behind the settees. I dipped into books I grabbed from the piles of random bric-a-brac that surrounded me. But my attention span was short, and my mind too unwilling-to-be-focused... And when I felt ready to continue, after what I believe must have been several days, I set off once again.

I moved on around bend after bend. And as I did so the lights became more frequent – stabbing, penetrating, all enveloping lights. I was sweating constantly. Cold, hot, grimy pores; my T-Shirt stuck to the groove of my spine, but I had to go on – like metal drawn to a distant invisible magnet.

I felt both at home and uncomfortable, free and happy within confined limits. I turned another slithery reptilian corner, and was greeted by three sofas: two rusty orange coloured ones and a brown one, and an office chair. And these seats and their arrangement was identical to all the others I had passed on the way – and identical to the relaxation point where I'd just come from. But they couldn't be the same, because that would mean that I'd gone in a circle – and I was certain I hadn't done that...

These relaxation points were identical but for the differences. Differences created by the distortion of time and perception – and, huh, possibly they were different...

I thought I saw her this time, stubbing out her cigarette – the girl from the dreams. But it was only a glimpse, if it was anything at all... I sat down on the brown sofa, bent forwards and picked up the lipstick-stained filter and remnant of cigarette from the ashtray on the coffee table. It was still warm – half smoked, stubbed out at pace and lopsided. She would have stabbed it down against the glass ashtray after the last in her stream of inhalations. Possibly a rapidly sucked-in nicotine overdrive of Kafkaesque anxiety had tipped her over to nausea. And the sickness on the tip of her tongue would have reminded her of her need to be somewhere else quickly.

I un-crumpled the cigarette and held it out in front of me to be examined. The lipstick was the same shade as all the other times – uncommon yet familiar. I sniffed it. It had no aroma of *her* to it, only that bonfiry smell that every aborted cigarette acquires.

I held it out in front of me once more – this time at arm's length. Filter upwards between my finger and thumb. It was like the sight of a gun, and I began aiming the bright lipstick-patch at the unknown and unseen blurredness, which I knew existed beyond my immediate… I switched my focus rapidly between the soiled filter and what was in its direct line – backwards and forwards, backwards and forwards. From filter to chest of drawers, to filter to pack of cards, to filter to record entitled 'Am Fenster' by City, back to filter and then to coffee machine.

I lay the half-smoked cigarette on the low thick wooden table, picked up a coin from the pile of coins next to the ashtray, and went around the back of the sofas to the coffee machine. I shoved the coin into the slot making a sharp downward motion as I let it go, to give it a little backspin. I listened to the mechanics wheeze into motion, and watched as the thin flow of dark steamy liquid poured into the cup. When it was ready, I took it and sat back down.

I eventually found my cigarette lighter in a pocket that I did not normally use for holding lighters. I picked up the cigarette, her cigarette, and lit it. It tasted impure, satisfactorily so. I inhaled and could feel the breath of experience and self-confidence descend into my scabby lungs. Someone else's saliva had given it a noticeable edge; it stood out from any normal cigarette. And I inhaled deeply and closed my eyes; I held the smoke in for as long as possible before blowing it slowly out between pursed lips. It made me feel closer to something that I was not convinced I wanted to feel closer to. So, I drank my coffee and the sweats began again. And sleep pulled slowly over me like the Turin shroud over an unshaved man…

She waved at me from the other end of a tunnel. She wore an outfit devoid of lines. I made my way tentatively towards her; the light was drawing me in. It was a bright light, a white light with a yellowy tinge. Then, as I was a third of the way along the tunnel, and, for the first time, I was beginning to make out some of the features on her face the tunnel swept up from under and around me. Whooshing all senses into a state of confusion. The tunnel with its dark greyish blurred indeterminate form rushed upwards into a growing monolith: a rapid construction of bricks to my left, one piling onto another like an enormous jenga tower.

I stood still and watched as the glassless windows formed. And before my consciousness could assimilate all that was happening a turreted gothic, blackened stone construction was towering in front of me. It should have had bats circling its high garrets, with Boris Karloff's hunched silhouette edging from left to right across the face of the building – it should have, but it didn't.

Then instantly, without knowing how I'd got there, I found myself cycling by this building through the deserted streets of Leipzig. But not the streets I had known on my first few days in Leipzig prior to my discovery of 'the shop'. These were streets from another time – the same and yet different. And it was dawn or dusk and the light was strange: there was a haunting glow to it, and it was slightly silvery hologrammatic.

There was not another person in sight. I was in a ghost town that was devoid of any ghosts – except for me. It looked cold, wintry, yet I felt warm… And as I rode past a Broiler Bar[14] I wished I'd written more poetry, more stuff from the soul… It felt as though I was hardly peddling, and although I seemed to be steering the rusty old sit-up-and-beg bike, it had a life of its own. I did not do it, but had I taken my feet off the pedals I had the impression that the bike would have kept on going of its own accord.

I cycled through the deserted streets of the city centre. Past the Intershop, around the Nikolaikirche[15], and in front of the Polish Information Bureau[16]. I whizzed along intrigued by my surroundings that were from another era. The streets were puddled, yet I did not make a splash. It was like being on a highly advanced fairground ride. The scenery was all around but I was in another place: on a bike on a stage maybe, a bike that did not move, similar to an exercise bike. My scenery was changing even if I was standing still; or, even if it *felt* as though I was standing still. And then there was a blinding flash of white light; a flash that sucked everything up into a nothingness. Not the kind of white that was a colour that was the opposite of black. It was much more basic than that – much purer, a whiteness that transcended the spectrum. That existed alone somehow. A whiteout.

The flash disappeared as suddenly as it had appeared and I found myself about 150 feet further along the road. I wanted to stop. I needed to stop after this momentary lapse of sensory perception. I used both brakes but it was not enough to completely halt the flow of the machine. I dragged my feet along the ground. Then I held both legs out to the side of me and sharply lowered them simultaneously to the ground. On their making contact with the road surface I pushed down and jumped backwards off the saddle. It took four or five stumbled steps before I came to a standstill. The bicycle careered onwards wobbling precariously before clattering into a three feet high wall.

I sat down on the wall with sweat pouring off me. My hair was matted and itchy. I scratched my head hard to loosen the hair from the scalp, and to let some air in. I buried my head in my hands and wondered when I would wake up. I looked over to the other side of the road. It was a wide road, multi-laned, with several tramlines running down its middle. And I realised I was looking over the wide inner ring road[17] that encircled Leipzig's city centre, across to the central station. It was a less glossy more antiquated version of the central station than the one I had arrived at all that time ago, but it was the same central station nonetheless. I recalled how my guidebook had informed me that Leipzig's train station is the largest in Europe, of the kind where the trains arrive and leave from the same direction.

To the left of the station, as I looked at it, was a side road. Parked up in this side road was a car, which represented the first sign of life I had come across in this place. It was facing away from me. And from my distance, and to my untrained eye, it looked like a Trabant. What a wonderful car the Trabbie was, I thought to myself: the Communists' version of the Mini. But instead of a scantily clad Twiggy photographed next to it, in my mind's eye I pictured Nina Hagen[18] sexily sprawled across its bonnet.

I threw a last glance over the bike before heading across this urban desert landscape towards the car. I felt as if I was being watched. Probably anyone in this faceless city would have felt the same. And it seemed to me that grey was the new sepia... I slowed as I neared. The light hit the back window in such a way as to reflect what was around and above the car, making it impossible to know if anyone was sitting inside. I took an elliptical route so as to approach the car sideways on. This meant that I would be able to see if the vehicle had an occupant, whilst maintaining a safe distance and hopefully remaining out of sight.

As I moved so did the reflection on the rear window: sky, building, lamppost, and road. I tentatively advanced along my circuitous route until I stood across the road from the car. And as the silver-grey washed skies brightened to give off a shiny mercury effulgent glow it became clear that it was dawn and not dusk. And once I'd edged far enough around I could see that there was no one in this black Trabant. Out of habit, although pointlessly, I looked right and left and right again before crossing to take a closer look.

I placed my hand on the bonnet to see if the car had been driven recently. It was inconclusive; the car certainly was not stone cold, but that could have been due to the day's mild beginnings. Momentarily I looked up at the widows in the Stalinesque skyscrapers to see if anyone was watching me. I could not see anyone, so I tried the driver's door, which un-clicked and smoothly opened. The interior smelt of stale smoke and warm plastic. The keys dangled from the ignition. I got in. I checked the rear view mirror and the wing mirror; I looked in front of me and over my shoulder. I turned the key and started her up. I revved slightly, although it was not needed. She turned over without a hiccough. There was a packet of Sprachlos cigarettes on the dashboard. I lit one up. I snatched a last glance around me, put her into first, eased off the clutch and pressed down on the throttle.

After about twenty minutes I reached the Autobahn and headed for Berlin. The surface of the motorway was made up of ten-meter long slats of concrete, with a ten-centimetre gap between each. This meant that as I drove along, a strange almost hypnotic rhythm was created. The 'fuzz' of the unsmooth concrete slabs was regularly broken up with a 'clack' sound as you drove over the gap. Fuzz, clack, fuzz, clack, fuzz, clack… The more quickly I went the closer together came the clacks. Until the sound became that of a steam train, then a helicopter. I didn't see another car on the Autobahn, and so I settled in to the monotony of motorway driving and allowed my thoughts to wander.

XV

I knew I was in a dream, but over the previous few weeks 'the shop' had also begun to be flooded with dreamlike qualities. And maybe I was experiencing the end! The end of ideology, the end of striving for the perfect day, and everything was being swallowed up by the frozen will of the faceless ones. History... possibly I was experiencing the end of history...

The shop had oozed and sweated its meaning to me, and then I'd spun into a dream.

For the last ten days or so I had experienced a sense of belonging and easiness that had soothed my waking hours. My diet was meagre, partly due to forgetfulness – I often just did not remember to eat – and partly due to lack of hunger. My intake and need for food had greatly diminished during this period. I had come across several well-stocked kitchens, but I could not always find them when I wanted to eat something. And when I did come across them I did not always feel like eating at that time, and just walked straight past them.

The woman, or at least the illusion of a woman, and the sweats and cramps that had blighted me had been somewhat of a preoccupation of mine. Nevertheless, my absorption with and by my surroundings was close to total. I was becoming part of 'the shop', and 'the shop' was becoming part of me. The line where one ended and the other began was no longer as determinable as it had been. I was becoming absorbed, and was content to facilitate this absorption. There was an underlying need in me to halt rational thought, and just be. I was guilty by association. I was an accessory to my own demise. I would not be content until the fripperies of my self were completely intermingled with the fascinations and obsessions of the shop, until the point where my id was comprehensively obliterated.

There was a white flash. It lasted a little longer this time, for several seconds. Long enough to focus on it and briefly consider its meaning. Long enough to be aware that its intense purity of light swallowed everything up; no single silhouette of any part of the surrounding landscape survived its all-intrusive brilliance. A crackle, I think there was a crackle that accompanied it – an electric crackle. A crackle similar to that given out by those purple contraptions that flies fly into in cafeterias... I also experienced a slight feeling of weightlessness this time. Maybe weightlessness is not quite right; it was more akin to the feeling you get in your stomach when you drop from a great height at speed. Seasickness mixed with bungee-jump dizziness.

I guessed I was further along the motorway once the light had subsided. Trees had replaced fields and it only took another twenty minutes before I reached Berlin... I saw nobody as I drove through the damp desolate streets. I didn't pass a single other car, neither moving nor stationary. There was not even any litter, a discarded cigarette packet, an old newspaper, a flier blowing in the wind – nothing. It was like an abandoned Wild West – Wild East – town, with the wind whistling down the street and the dejected clanging sound of the old swinging church bell. It was the Socialist Wild West, the egalitarian hill country, the Communist Klondike, where the panning for truth had long since ceased. Even if unknown to most, there was 'still gold in them tha hills'. And I had the feeling I was the far-out stranger riding into town.

There were curtains in apartment windows and clothes in shop windows, sometimes accompanied by the sign Unverkäufliches Beratungsmuster[19]. I drove under the large bulbous radio tower, through to Alexander Platz[20], where I pulled up to light another cigarette. I had to pull up because the matches had fallen to the floor. I lit up, opened the window, and wondered what to do next.

I checked the glove compartment. I was sure, however, that in the book about cars that I had found in the shop, it stated that Trabants didn't have glove compartments. But I chose to ignore this anomaly and shuffled through the contents. A scrunched up empty packet of cigarettes and numerous official looking pieces of paper were piled on top of an A5 size leather zip-up folder.

I flicked my ash into the ashtray and opened the folder. Inside were one hundred and fifteen East German Marks, some Genex Geld[21] to the value of thirty Marks, a cash point card[22], some miscellaneous receipts, an envelope with a stamp on it but with no address, and most intriguingly of all a driving license. The little rectangle where the photograph should have been was empty, although it was clear from the bumpy paper sinews that at one time a photograph had been there.

I looked at the line where 'Name' was written – I was just able to make out the letter 'C' before there was a blinding blanket of white light that engulfed the whole city. Only a flash this time, with no crackle or sense of weightlessness. And when the light had given way to the rain-threatening morning skies once again, I found myself parked a little way further along the pavement. I was no more than ten metres further on. But the other strange thing was that the folder was back in the glove compartment, the matches were on the floor again, and when I opened the packet of Sprachlos to spark another one up, there were the same number of cigarettes as there had been when I left Leipzig.

As I reached down to pick up the matches to light the cigarette that hung loosely from my lips, my hand came into contact with a cylindrical object. I picked it up along with the matches. It was a lipstick. I opened it; it was the same peculiar shade that had been on the stubbed out cigarettes in the shop.

I lit up and put the match in the ashtray, and then let my index finger rummage around amongst the overflowing ash. Underneath the layers of ash were three cigarette butts emblazoned with the distinctive shade of the woman's lipstick. I opened the leather folder, riffling through the same things that had been there the first time: the cash point card, several receipts, some Genex

Geld, one hundred and twenty-five East German Marks, an envelope – this time with an address on it but the stamp and most of the post-mark had been torn away – and the driving licence. My gaze went directly to the section containing the personal details; the photograph was still missing.

Flash. The flashes were less perturbing to me now. They had become an intrinsic part of my whole plight, and no longer a threatening jolt that dragged me away from the state I was in.

I was ready for this last flash. I had predicted it. I knew it was going to occur right at that very moment. This time I was only five metres further forward. The cigarette packet was completely full and the matches lay next to them on the dashboard. I picked the lipstick up from the floor, the colour was the same but unlike before it had hardly been used. I squeezed a cigarette out of the soft packet and popped it between my lips. I lit it and used the dead match to prod the contents of the ashtray. One lipstick-stained butt sat under the pile of ash. I coaxed it out and rubbed the ash from it on the passenger seat; and with my other hand I opened the window a quarter of the way down, leaned back in my chair, let my head fall backwards and blew a lung full of smoke up against the ceiling of the car...

I put the lipstick in my pocket and started the car. I noticed that the tank was full, despite the distance I'd driven from Leipzig... I drove out of Alexander Platz and headed towards the Berlin Wall[23]. I looked either side of me as I moved silently through the both bleak and yet somehow comfortingly retro streets. I thought how it could all have been a film set – it had that eerie unlived in cardboard cut-out quality about it.

I approached Checkpoint Charlie[24] slowly. There was nobody around, nobody in the watchtowers, and the barriers were up. I drove through at 10 km/hour, taking my time to absorb as much as I could. For, dream or no dream, what I was experiencing was fascinating. How many people had the chance to drive through Checkpoint Charlie, I wondered. Not that I should get carried away, for I had no way of knowing how much of it was accurate.

I did not really know what to do, just drive around and wait until I woke up seemed as good a plan as any. I pulled the car over a little way around the corner from Checkpoint Charlie. I looked around me but there was no one on this side of The Wall – the West side – either. The colours were brighter on this side, trashier, even if they'd been somewhat dulled by the rain and the dream. I spent a few moments examining the graffiti on The Berlin Wall: Politics, love, sex, music, and freedom – just about covered everything. *Wer will das die Welt so bleibt wie sie ist, der will nicht das sie bleibt*[25] was scrawled next to a painting of a tall black tree. And next to the tree was a picture of a white Trabant smashing through The Wall with a smiling man sitting in the driving seat.

A little further along was a caricatured portrayal of the American president with a dartboard for a heart; the unseen thrower had scored one hundred and fifty. I smiled and as I did so the ash from my cigarette fell onto the seat between my legs, and I swiped it off with the back of my hand... I pulled the handbrake up and got out of the car, putting the keys into my back pocket. There was no need to take the keys with me, but habit dictated that I must.

I took a stroll along the pavement by The Wall. I crossed the road and thought I heard a wisp of Aeolian music coming from the distance somewhere. As I advanced along the opposite pavement, I discovered the source of these mellifluent stirrings: the wind was squeezing its way down metal pipes and through mechanical tubes of battered looking construction equipment. The equipment was idly festering in a small yard, which clearly belonged to industrial folk.

From the side of the road I was on I could see the dome of the radio tower and some of the higher roofs and houses in the Russian Sector[26]. A puddle jumped up and clung to my shoe. I ignored it, and consequently my foot remained dry. I turned around to look at what I could see of the entrance to Checkpoint Charlie, and saw the same sign that had been in the shop, which informed anyone who approached that they would soon be leaving the American Sector.

I sat on a wall and looked at The Wall. Facing me was a picture of Breznev and Honecker French kissing. And I just sat there, stared, and thought... My mind roamed from one subject to another. There was no structure to my mental wanderings, and little effort on my part to give them any. I simply sat and passively let them pulse in and out of my consciousness: a drainpipe, a puddle, my wet shoe that felt dry to the touch, cigarettes, the car, the DDR, The Wall, industrial machinery, the woman, lipstick, makeup, the zephyr on my face, coffee, coffee machines, sugar, milk, a grillette[27], the woman, the breeze dancing through the construction equipment, David Bowie in Berlin, music, Quietschpappe[28], the woman, the shop, lipstick, time, vague blurry memories of childhood, semiology, construction, deconstruction, time, non-linear, The Wall, the car, the lipstick, the folder, the woman, the driving licence, the woman…

These thoughts siphoned their way through the nooks and crannies of my mind. And I was merely an onlooker as these thoughts wafted through me on a current of air on their way to some other place. I felt the way I had felt in the shop: my identity was redefining itself. A human being dissolved, only to be rebuilt in another form. And yet none of this seemed to be happening to *me*. Or, at least, it felt as if it was happening to another me, a distant me – a me that I could sit back and observe.

My attention was drawn to a puddle in the gutter. I watched as the breeze rippled its surface, and how, when the wind died down, it would return to its mirror-like stillness. Then there was a clap, like a thunderclap, which shook me out of my torpor. I looked up and saw as the world began to realign: angles, angles and lines, no curves, only angles and lines. The sky was a patchwork of differing shades of greys, whites, and smoky blues. The sweeping strokes of the hip-hop writing on The Wall transformed into a thick heavy formal typeface; the faces of the Presidents and politicians had become robotic, squared off angular versions of their former selves. The road and driveways were T-junctions and right angles. And the wheels on the Trabant were square. Everything had transformed into a psychotic's cubist nightmare.

At this point my thoughts became rampant. I stood up with persecuted eyes, looking zombie-like and mutoidinal. I stared into some ill-defined void and stumbled in the direction of the car. A third of the way across the road my foot hit a bump, or a rock, or something. I tried to stagger onwards but the upper half of my body was toppling forwards faster than my feeble legs could keep up. And as I crunched into the sodden road surface I saw white – white through plastic, white through glass. It was a neon white, which enveloped me and clung onto me. It was the eternal burning of an electric candle; it was a white light in a white night, with the constant buzz of time elapsing…

Once the whiteness had receded I rolled over onto my side to begin what I knew would be the energy-sapping exercise of pushing myself back upright. I heaved myself into a sitting position, and as I did so a gust of chill breeze hit me and made me shiver. Then from the corner of my eye I saw something white flapping towards me. I turned quickly; ready to fend off whatever it was.

And as my face turned to the wind, a damp and cold flier slapped onto my right cheek. I gasped – both from the shock of the strange, and the discomfort from the sodden sheet of paper hitting me like a lady with a morning-dew-damp glove whose honour had been besmirched.

I peeled the A5 throwaway carefully from my face. I wiped my cheek dry with my sleeve and placed the sheet on my knee. I bent forwards to be sure of what I was about to read.

Time is short

There is no cure… not yet!

Go with it …

This is the past, created by the mind.

And at the bottom of the flier I thought I saw what looked like the signature of my uncle… Then I blinked; I blinked repeatedly. I raised my arms up, beckoning to the skies like a fire and brimstone preacher; and I began rubbing my eyes with the heels of my hands. After a couple of minutes I removed my hands from my face, blinked again, and peered back down at the flier.

Time is short

There is no cure for listening to insipid music.

Well… there is one cure:

Go with it, and come and join us

At The Goldfish bar tonight.

Come and listen to the group 'Maybe'

21:00h till late; free entry.

I must have passed out... When I came to I felt groggy and drained. My head was lolling to one side on my shoulder and it took me several moments before my faculties reached a sufficient level of awareness to realise that I was once again cycling madly along the streets of Leipzig...

And so it was, that each time I managed to lull myself into some kind of manageable security, *bang*, everything altered. Each time I became happy with my surroundings they disappeared. Each time I found answers to my questions, or not even answers just the formulations of the right questions, the questions were no longer relevant. Or, at least, these questions were superceded by other more pressing questions. Or possibly, just possibly, I was experiencing the final obliteration of self...

Whoooosh – the bike took me along at its own pace. The rain's residue still languished on the ground, but the skies were clearing. I let the surroundings pass before my eyes and I stopped thinking. And the bike careered on, weaving its spindly frame through the ancient market streets of Leipzig; over the cobbled surfaces that surrounded the Nikolaikirche, and then back out onto the Inner Ring – retracing the same route as before.

I spied the soulless Trabant still parked in the side road next to the station. This entire locus, I thought to myself, was a shell devoid of life and empty of emotion. It was a moribund shadow inhaling its last breaths of hope, mournfully puling about what could have been. And yet, this behemoth remained defiantly proud as it gazed down upon the fountainheads of tomorrow.

But it was nevertheless a contrast to how this place must have once been, and to how the shop now was: the shop was packed with memories, feelings, and trinkets full of history. And I realised that this land – the land of wet streets, bright flashes, and half cycled journeys – only existed because I existed. Without my presence it would cease to be...

The bicycle eventually came to a sudden halt in front of Die Runde Ecke[29]... I was shaken by the bike's unannounced emergency stop, and took a few moments to gather myself. I then looked up at the imposing entrance to the building. As I did so a coruscation of a memory came rushing back to me: on my second or was it third full day in the city, I visited Die Runde Ecke building. When I was there it was a museum, but in DDR times it had been the Stasi[30] headquarters. I recall walking through the post room, with its machines for steaming open letters and gluing them back together again. And then the ironing machine that removed the wrinkles made by the steaming machine.

A little further along was the room the guards had called 'room 1-0-1'. Whether this had been just to frighten the prisoners, or for the guards' own amusement – or… well, or because there truly was a close parallel between their room 1-0-1 and the 'real' room 1-0-1 – was not clear. A room from which possibly the only way to escape was to close one's eyes and roam freely amongst the wanderings of one's dreams…

I alighted from the bike and headed for the steps that led up to the fifteen feet high wooden entrance doors of Die Runde Ecke. My legs felt unsteady, as if I had been sitting or standing in the same place for a long time… My legs buckled and I went down. This time the flash was cold. Brilliant white and ice cold. The duration of this sheet of whiteness could have been anything from a few seconds to, I don't know, a few days. And I must have passed out as I hit the ground.

I found myself half way along the dark steamy tunnel. She stood at the other end in a pool of light, a pool of frosted light. She was standing sideways on, yet with her head facing away. She wore some kind of jumpsuit. I hurried along, my legs were strong, but the floor was uneven. I recognised her: her form, her clothes. I had seen her before but I could not remember where. I needed to see her face close up, with that distinctive lipstick on the lips it belonged to. The light was dimming and the tunnel did not seem to be getting any shorter. I speeded up, but it made no difference – I remained in the middle of the tunnel.

I thought if she turned around I might be able to make out her features. Merely a momentary glimpse might trigger off a memory, a memory that seemed to be pivotal to so much. The light was fading fast and I gave one last attempt to reach her. I propelled myself forwards with as much vigour as I could. And all the while she was standing as still as an upright corpse. The last thing I saw was that the collar on her outfit was turned up, but only limply so – half-cocked with nonchalant indifference.

XVI

I woke up drenched and shivering. My head was resting on one arm of the brown sofa, my feet crossed on the other. The neon strips bled their unforgiving light over everything. I blinked long and slow: a sign of resignation and an aid to concentration. I pulled out my mirror-cup from my jacket pocket. I looked gaunt and pale, almost bluish pale. The coffee was cold and murky, the coins were scattered and the cigarettes lay cremated and ashen. I sat up and rolled myself a cigarette. I rolled hastily as though I had not smoked for ages. My hands trembled, with cold and desperation. I lit up and inhaled deeply, expectant of the nicotine fix that I longed for. I felt nothing. The tip of the cigarette looked hotter and brighter but I felt no smoke satisfyingly descend into my lungs. I exhaled and saw the fumes pour out like smoke from a chimney, and still I felt nothing. I tried again: inhale exhale. Nothing.

The exhalation was nothing more than the puff of breath on a chill winter's morning. I stubbed it out in disgust. Its end was as rapid as its beginning, and I stared at it for a moment, doubled up and extinguished. A contorted corpse that I had no further use for. I heard a click, clickety-click, and saw a flicker as one of the mighty tubes of light gave up the ghost. Maybe I was a ghost; maybe she was. Not a phantom so much as a ripple of a memory. A lingering thought that was neither *here* nor *there*; or a trapped recollection that could not yet freely move on to the next plane.

I went to the coffee machine, popped a coin in the slot, and pressed the button for an Im Nu[31] with extra sugar. It was piping hot. I cupped both my hands around it to extract as much heat as I could. But it made little, if any, difference to the cold within my bones.

How much longer was this going to go on for? My memories of former times were faint now, but this was probably due to my fever… I would be fine again in a few days. I had just caught a chill. Berlin had been windy and damp, and riding around on bikes in the early morning cannot have helped.

I finished off my Im Nu and headed inwards towards the centre of the shop. The route was carpeted once again, sumptuous bouncy and red. I looked down and watched my feet sink a little with each step I took. I slowed down and pretended that there was little gravity, exaggeratedly lifting my legs as high as I could with knees bent. As each knee reached its highest position – with my arms waggling out to either side to keep my balance – I extended my leg out in front of me lowering it leisurely until my heel made contact with the thick carpet. With my heel on the ground, I watched as I unhurriedly lowered the rest of my foot bit by bit. I paid close attention to how the carpet gave way as more and more of the sole of my foot sank into its surface.

I repeated this Jupiter-walking over and over again. I was fascinated by how the indentations that my feet made left no 'memory' once they had gone. My foot on the carpet left everything squashed and flat; once I lifted it the whole area returned to its former self. Not a trace remained. It became a seemingly untouched place – a pretend virgin with a synthetic hymen.

Whilst transfixed by my slow motion prowling, a realisation struck me. A realisation that transformed into concern… Who would know I had ever been here? If I died, what footprints would I leave? The tide was a springy carpet, which washed over any disturbance I may have made in the sand…

I walked on with urgency, time was running out, and I had to reach the centre of the shop. I felt weak but the adrenalin drove me on. I passed a section with clothes racks either side of the aisle.

I stopped and ripped my jacket off, and pulled my T-Shirt and jumper over my head. I flung the sodden garments to the ground and flicked through the rows of second-hand clothes. The first things that I came across that vaguely appeared to be my size were a long-sleeved version of the DDR national football team's white away jersey[32], and a blue FDJ[33] jacket.

I picked up my jumper and gave my torso a wipe to absorb some of the thin film of sweat that covered my body. I put my newly found clothes on; they were cold but dry. After the fifth rack of clothes there was an oblong trestle table that had been painted matt black. It was covered with accessories: plastic handbags, cigarette holders, cigarette cases, bead necklaces, tie clips, and an array of spectacles, sunglasses, and glasses cases. I picked out a pair of black tinted glasses with a thin metal scaffold for a frame. The lenses were oval: amusingly, one lens was horizontal whilst the other was upright.

Kitted out and dry I hurried on. I had only gone a few steps, however, before I realised I had forgotten to empty the contents of my old jacket pockets. I went back and rummaged through my six pockets: two on the inside and four on the outside. In one of the inside pockets was a silver coloured metal petrol lighter that someone had once given me, but I could not recall who; and in the top right outside pocket was a small blunt 4B pencil and a torn off corner of a piece of paper with a sketch of a die on it – the number 4 was on top and the 1 was facing to the front. The other outside pocket held my tobacco pouch and four packets of cigarette papers, one of which was empty but had a phone number with a British dialling code written on its inside flap.

On turning the next corner I saw another of the shop's relaxation points. As with the others, it was set a little way back from the aisle, with three settees around a small wooden table. But this time, instead of there being a hot drinks machine behind the back settee, there was a telephone kiosk. Hanging from one of the metal shelves that was next to the telephone kiosk was a painting. I walked slowly towards the knee-high table unable to take my eyes from the picture. It was beautiful. It looked like something Salvador Dali would have painted, but for some reason I didn't think it was one of his… A giant eggshell, broken in two, either side of an expanse of water, was held in place by scaffolding. Rising on the horizon, as though emerging from the water, was the yellow sun looking as if it was the yolk of the egg. And in the foreground was a small figure running away from the sun.

As I stared mesmerised by this powerful image, I thought that possibly the figure running towards the viewer was me... My legs bumped into something and I looked down. I had reached the table. On the table was a cream-coloured satchel. I was unable to stop thinking about the meaning of the painting; nevertheless, I absent-mindedly picked up the satchel and looked inside. Inside were probably a couple of hundred pages of hand-written paper. I slung the satchel over my shoulder, telling myself that I would consider the contents when I had more time.

I took the telephone number out of my pocket and made my way round to the kiosk. I dialled.

"Hello?" said the startled female voice.

"Hello," I replied.

"Yes, can I help you?"

"Erm... I think I'm in trouble."

"Oh dear... Is that by any chance the late Dr Palmer's nephew?"

"Um," I affirmed.

"Don't worry... You're doing the right thing."

I think it must have been after another couple of minutes of talking that I let the phone drop out of my hand and swing by its cord. I felt weak, I had been sidetracked for too long, and I had the sense that time was my adversary...

As I hurried on along the aisle, I began to wonder if the telephone conversation had really happened at all. The thought momentarily perturbed me, but before I could allow it to fester, I was distracted by another light spluttering and dying above my head. The shop was getting dimmer, as if the whole place was shutting down; and I could sense that time was getting short... I rushed along the weaving path, red-eyed and perspiring. I was probably running a high temperature, but had no time for self-indulgence. I passed metal shelves on either side of me containing a variety of kitchen appliances. After swinging a sharp left I passed boxes full of sports equipment. And I kept on going – until I reached a T-junction.

A white wall was facing me – a white wall that spanned from right to left. Very shortly after turning right, in what I considered to be the direction of the centre, the shelves and boxes to the right of this pathway were replaced by a white wall; a white wall that sloped up from the ground. Once the wall had reached its final height, and I then had a wall on either side of me, the white passageway was about twice my height.

The flooring of this pathway had also changed. It too was now white: white painted concrete, the same colour and texture as the two walls. I speeded up again, from a fast walk to a jog. Another strip light gave several sorrowful flickers in a lacklustre attempt to extend its life before finally fizzling out. The perspiration was dripping off me. The sole of my left shoe must have been wearing thin for each time I plonked my foot down my heel hurt. Not a great pain, but enough to know there was little, if any, material between my foot and the hard passageway.

After running for several minutes the path widened slightly. I turned a 90° corner to the left, and was confronted with two identical white doors with silver handles. I stopped and looked from door to door, considering my options. Not that there was really that much to consider. Either I took the right door or I took the left one. Nevertheless, I must have spent several minutes standing there contemplating the importance of my decision. I knew I was close, I could feel it. Possibly one route would take me straight to the middle whilst the other would simply lead me away, maybe back round into the shop.

I was aware that time was against me, and felt very weak now that I had stopped; and I knew I was dehydrated… For no particular reason I plumped for the left door. I took the ten steps required to approach what could possibly turn out to be my destiny. Deliberately I reached out my left arm and placed my hand on the chill metal handle, and cautiously applied downward pressure. The lock clicked and I felt like a burglar in a foreign land. I tentatively pushed the door as another neon bulb overhead gave way to the darkness.

I was standing in a shadow land. The shop was closing and the only way was forward. I pushed a little harder against the spring-loaded door and a shaft of white light flooded through, over, and around me. I let my exhausted mind bathe in its inviting illumination. I walked through, and I knew there was no going back.

The door closed behind me and I found myself in a completely white corridor. It was similar to the one I had come from except this one was completely enclosed. The ceiling mirrored the walls and the floor. With the absence of gravity I would have been unable to tell down from up. And I felt like a spy in an alcove, all surreptitious and unannounced.

The light drew me in, and the rush had gone. My head was lighter now and the sweats had disappeared. A lighter way of thinking, less garbled and coded. Less hindered by questions and reasons; less tempered by the weight of self. I walked a stately path through the corridor's glow. Round the bends that held no secrets, swaying along to the rhythm of the distant hum. Words and thoughts were no longer a hindrance to my advancement. Nor, I felt, would the dreams bother me again. The temporariness of it all, or at least the feeling of the temporariness of it all, had vanished. No longer did I walk a thin waking tightrope that barely separated my tentative reality from the confusions and convolutions in my head.

Nothing distinguished one part of the corridor from the next. The light was uniform and the surfaces were interchangeable. My feet beat out a regular step in 4/4 time, with no breaks or bridges, no hooks or melodies – just the simple marching time of someone with a purpose.

I was not sure how long I had been walking when I saw the door, hypnotised, as I had been, by the all pervasiveness of nothingness and the easiness of my mind. It was a long straight stretch of passageway that signalled the arrival of the door. Somehow I knew it was the last door: the door that divided what had been with what had to be. And I knew that there was some crooked inevitability that permeated all of this. I just had not been able to figure out what it was. There were too many gaps; too many clues without structure. Too many signs that floated in the air severed from their umbilical cords too soon, devoid of life and without meaning.

Calmness wrapped me up in its gentle talons, and I was ready. I drew a long deep breath and released it with slow intention. I pushed against a silver panel in the centre of the door, which was the same shape and size as a letterbox, but perpendicular. I pushed with the palm of my right hand. I pushed a little harder. I heard the slight whoosh of hydraulics, as the door lifted up and away from me. And as the door slowly rose, the shaft of blinding white light engulfed me.

I edged tentatively forwards like a blind man feeling his way. And then with my arms outstretched I merged with the incandescence. No object impeded my way. A thought, detached and honourable, pushed for prominence in my psyche: I had forgotten to pay the shop owner for all the bits and pieces I had picked up on my meanderings through the shop. I grabbed a fistful of currency from my right trouser pocket, turned, and slung it as forcefully as I could through the remaining gap under the door. Coins clattered everywhere: against the door, against the wall, and thankfully through the ever decreasing strip of space that was left between the door and the floor. The banknotes too ended up going everywhere – some making it hardly any distance at all, fluttering weightless to my feet, others, that had managed to cling themselves around a few pieces of nickel, made it through to where I hoped the proprietor would eventually find them.

I turned to face the interrogatory light source once more. I heard the unhurried workings of the door sigh shut, and the light began to subside. And once the light had finally reached an acceptable level I began to examine my new surroundings. I was in a box, a white box. All six surfaces were identical. Even the wall behind me showed no trace of there ever having been a door there; although I guessed that had I bothered to inspect the surface more closely I would have detected a little space between where the wall ended and the door began. I went over to the corner and sat down with my knees up to my chin. I folded my arms, placed them on top of my knees, rested my head on top of them, and waited for something to happen.

I noticed that the humming sound was a little louder than it had been... And then there was a flash.

I came to, lying on the floor of the shiny bathroom. The shower was running, spraying its jet through a cloud of steam. I raised myself to a sitting position, rubbed my eyes, and wondered. I was naked. I looked around but I couldn't see any clothes anywhere. I stood up and went over to the gleaming mirror above the sink. I stared at the face staring back at me. I looked OK. No, I looked good – healthy, well-preserved, with no bags, and closely shaved.

I transferred my gaze to the torrents of hot water invitingly cascading down. I made my way over and got in. As I stood under this electric waterfall, with my eyes closed and my head raised, allowing its bombardment to softly sting my face and plummet down over the rest of my body, I realised that I looked too good. I looked too fresh. I had never looked this good. I looked like a perfect re-creation of the healthiest fittest possible version that my self could have been if I had lived my life under laboratory conditions. I looked ad perfect, false and unbelievable, with a smile that was too straight and white. It was a smile that had little to do with the real world, and had nothing to do with me... I did not want to look game-show-host-hygienic or sit-com sterile. I wanted to look lived in, a little scruffy around the edges, with late-night eyes and skin one size too large. I wanted to look like me: happy and haggard.

I got out of the perfect shower and wrapped the perfectly fluffy sky blue towel around me. I took another few moments to examine myself in the mirror. I looked, I don't know... too clean living, too well-preserved, pickled. I bared my teeth and a perfect toothpaste ad smiled back. I dripped my way into the bedroom. Outside the window it was daytime, it was warm, it looked like summer. The sun poured in through the large expanse of window – the rays skating over the black satin sheets on the king-size bed, ending up in a pool of light on the far wall to my left.

I sauntered over to the window. I knew this place – the layout, the feeling, even the broken clock on the bedside table signified something to me. But it was all nothing more than drip-fed memories. I un-clicked the latch, opened the window wide, and inhaled the freshly mown summer fragrances that lethargically wafted in with the dust particles on the warm currents of air.

A little way up the street two mid-elderly gentlemen were engaged in lively conversation. Laughing and gesticulating fervently, they were too absorbed in their exchanges to notice the elderly white-haired woman arrive. She tapped the one wearing the crimson velvet jacket on the shoulder. He turned, smiled, and put his arm loosely around her waist. His free hand, which was palm up and slightly tilted, he moved backwards and forwards between the woman and the other man two or three times. And I surmised that introductions were being made.

They seemed happy enough idling away their time in the mid morning sunshine. I too, in that brief absent-minded moment, was happy enough just to idly watch them and let the sun beat its unfiltered rays against my face. As I was about to turn away from this scene of inch high shorn lawns and suburban tranquillity, I saw an elegant woman in a wheelchair coming along the pavement. She was waving frantically. I naturally assumed that she was making her presence known to the three people on the other pavement. As she continued in my direction, however, I gradually realised that not only did she appear to be waving to me, but that she was the spitting image of my grandmother...

I quickly ducked down out of sight. She really had looked exactly like my grandmother – but my grandmother had died when I was twelve. I crouched down under the window for several minutes to gather my thoughts. I then crawled away until I had reached an adequate distance so as not to be seen as I stood back up. I then nonchalantly returned to the window as though nothing had happened.

When I reached the window, all four were engaged in animated discourse. I watched for a little while – I liked to watch things in the street. And I concentrated on my grandmother's double for a while. Then I went and sat on the bed and thought that if everybody had a doppelganger, where was mine... The bed slid against my body – black and smooth, and I fell asleep.

I must have slept for the entire day, for when I awoke it was dark outside. Whether the sound had been in my dream, or had come from outside and filtered into my dream, I could not be sure. Either way, I had awoken to the sound of a siren, similar, I thought, to that of an air raid siren, or a factory siren. I switched the bedside lamp on and went over to the still open window.

It was a warm night, but there was *nothing* to be seen. Not a single thing. Everything was pitch black. The street, the houses, even the sky was devoid of celestial bodies. No moon, no stars, no clouds, only darkness; a black ceiling on the world. And I stood there peering out at this lifeless universe for a while, trying to distinguish forms amongst the emptiness. I felt that I was in a house floating in space, a space devoid of anything but me. And as I gazed into the infinite darkness, an overwhelming sense of loneliness acupunctured me all over, and I began to cry…

With wet cheeks I went over to the other side of the bed and plugged the radio alarm clock into the wall. The clock momentarily flashed 00:00 before settling on 33:02. I fiddled with the dial trying to tune the radio in. But from end to end there was nothing. The only sound over the airwaves was a distant electrical hum, like a thousand bumblebees caught in a trap. I crawled under the sheets, turned onto my side and went back to sleep.

When I eventually awoke, the sun was shining on another sparklingly pristine new day. I went over to the window, as I felt I'd done before. The two gentlemen were there again chatting away in almost the identical spot as before. And as far as I could remember they had the same clothes on. And then I spied the same elderly lady walking along the pavement. She also had the same outer layers on. She discreetly approached the crimson-jacketed gentleman and lightly prodded him in the back. He turned and, on seeing who the finger belonged to, affectionately put his arm around her waist and gently coaxed her inwards to form a triangle between the three of them.

I felt uneasy and lost. And I knew that on one level or another I was trapped. Like a hamster in a cage or a goldfish in a sushi bar, I was running, swimming, running around in circles…

I found some clothes that fitted me in the wardrobe – a pair of black trousers and a brown shirt – I put them on and went back into the bathroom to clean my teeth. I had this strange feeling that I was being watched. I came out of the spotless bathroom and went back over to close the window. The two men were on their own once again chatting away passionately about something or other. It was like watching some looped film – with the same trapped moments repeating themselves. I gave this inexplicably familiar room a final look before going through the door next to the bathroom.

I found myself on a landing looking down over an open-plan living room. It was a very light modern room, with windows that reached from the floor to the ceiling, and from the wall containing the fireplace on the right to the front door and the opening to what looked like the kitchen to the left. Before going downstairs, I decided to take a look in the room at the end of the landing.

As I approached the white door with the silver handle, I heard a whirring hum that appeared to be coming from inside the room. It was an electrical sound a little like the sound that a far off chain saw would make; or possibly it was more like the sound of a food mixer. I cautiously turned the handle and pushed the door. It did not open easily due to the thick carpet underneath, a carpet that by the looks of it had been newly laid.

A bright white light poured out and I went in. At first it was difficult to make anything out. After a minute or so, the light subsided enough for me to see that I was inside a box, a large white box. The hum was louder now. I made my way over to the left hand corner of this white cube, which in some odd way was also not a complete stranger to me… I sat down with my back against the wall, pulled my legs up to my chest, rested my arms on top, and lay my head on top of my arms. I closed my eyes as the hum got louder and waited for something to happen…

XVII

(Part I)

Sandra climbed down the stairs and alighted from the number 27. It was only a twenty minute walk from the bus stop to her work. Countryside, leafy streets, and grassy knolls surrounded her workplace, which was on the outskirts of the outskirts of town.

It was a high-security establishment. And every morning she had to go through the same old rigmarole of showing her pass, getting her fingerprints electronically scanned, and her iris photographed. After which she would proceed through outer gates and inner doors before reaching her section of work, where she could finally relax.

Prior to getting the job, she had been given a questionnaire to complete, full of questions concerning her family history and personal life. She had also been given forms to sign, which stated that she agreed not to reveal any information about the work that was being carried out at the compound...

"Good Morning Bill."

"Morning Sandra. Good weekend?"

"Yes thanks." Sandra handed over her pass, which Bill returned as soon as he'd scanned it.

Sandra made her way across the compound whilst being fully aware of the camera on the laboratory's roof, which was following her as she crossed the quadrangle. She did not work in the laboratory herself, yet had to go through the same entrance as the laboratory workers… Her job was to constantly monitor the readings, notify the specialists if the thermostats needed regulating, and generally keep a well-trained eye out for anything untoward. She also had to greet any new arrivals and make them feel as comfortable as she could.

Even after having worked there for nearly two years, Sandra still had to pinch herself when she thought about how fortunate she was. She was earning nearly double that of her previous job, and the work was simpler. It was still a bit of a mystery to her how she had got the job in the first place. But she did not want to tempt fate by questioning things too much, for she knew that opportunities like these had to be grabbed when they presented themselves. Sure, it was a little boring at times, but the money more than made up for that…

What had happened was that once she'd left university with her doctorate, she'd got a job working in laboratories thirty miles away to the east. She had been working in her own field of expertise: rapid single flux quantum digital electronics technology. And despite having been content in her job, she had been ready for something new.

She was approached at her place of work one day and asked if she might be interested in a vacancy that had come up. And though the exact nature of the work wasn't divulged to her until some time later, she was told there were significant overlaps with her specialism in the area of superconductivity.

When she did finally discover what she was getting herself into she didn't know how she felt about it. It all seemed so bizarre. And one of the most bizarre aspects of all, as Sandra saw it, was that at its core was a fundamental contradiction: science was crucial to everything they did there, and yet, equally crucial was belief, or faith. The most unscientific of notions was *as* important in her new place of work as science was. And she had to admit that within the walls of that compound the one could not exist without the other. At least not until science advanced enough… As for the specific details of what they were doing, she simply didn't think about it.

Sandra placed the palm of her right hand against the screen on the wall. She waited several seconds until the large red letters appeared, spelling out the word 'Authorised'. The door clicked unlocked and she pushed her way through. She walked along the white passageway and turned left at the end. She went a little way until she came to a set of double doors. She stared up into the camera above the door, and when the buzzer sounded she placed her key in the lock and turned. She walked through, and the doors shut with a hydraulic swoosh behind her.

This was her little domain; this was where she had worked for the best part of two years. To the left was her office. Three of the four sides of her office consisted of a waist high white wall, on top of which were reinforced glass panels for the rest of the way up to the ceiling. In her office she had a desk, with an internal telephone on it, a swivel chair, and a few shelves. Most importantly of all was the control panel, which was to the right of her desk.

It was the control panel, with its monitors and continual rolling readouts, which she had to keep her eyes on. Not that she had to watch it every minute of every hour, but she had to remain vigilant just in case of any sudden changes or fluctuations in the readings. Not that there ever were any. And because there weren't, Sandra no longer scrutinised the readings as closely as she once had.

To the right was the wall of glass that separated the hallway from the Long Room where all the separate individual cubicles hung one after another in column after column. And a little past her office was the Relaxation Zone where, for example, she took her breaks, or where new arrivals waited and had a cigarette if they wanted.

The Relaxation Zone consisted of three sofas around a low thick wooden coffee table. Sandra bent over and picked up a token from one of the two piles that was on the coffee table. She went and unlocked her office and got her coffee mug from her desk. She left the door of her office open and walked around to the coffee machine that was located against the wall behind the sofas. She placed her mug in the little compartment, popped the token in the slot, pressed the button, and waited. The machine clunked into action and soon she had a steaming hot cup of coffee in her hands. She walked back around the sofas, placed her mug on the coffee table, and sat down on the sofa that faced the cubicles. She took a swig from her mug and blankly stared through the soundproof glass ahead. She felt around in her bag for her packet of cigarettes. She found it, took a cigarette out, put it between her lips, and lit it with the box of matches that lay on the coffee table.

At the end of the corridor to the left, just past the toilets and shower room, was the Medication Room; which remained unmanned, except for when a new client was due... Sandra sipped her coffee and stubbed out her cigarette. She immediately lit up another one whilst focusing on the frosted glass cubicles that stood in columns behind the wall of glass that ran the whole length of the Long Room. She was not thinking about anything in particular, merely gazing emptily at what was directly in front of her.

On days like today the journey into work was fine, it was with the damp and frosty winter mornings that Sandra had a problem. Never mind needing half an hour to relax on her arrival at work, on cold mornings it would take her at least that time to thaw out. The twenty minute walk on the final stretch of her journey was the worst part on winter mornings, and the best part at this time of the year. She would pass the duck pond, which had a little island in the middle with a hut on it, next to which was a sign that read: Duckingham Palace. A sign that had not failed to make her smile for the first six months of her job, but which she now found to be twee.

A quarter of a mile after the duck pond Sandra would take a left and cross a field. At the other end of the field, hidden between a row of oak trees, was a style. She would climb over the style into the adjacent field, in the middle of which was the compound. She would walk up to the tall perimeter fence, with its spotlights and surveillance cameras, and make her way along the narrow concrete path which followed the fence all the way around, until she arrived at the main gate...

As Sandra was enjoying her morning ritual of coffee and cigarettes, she noticed that the strip light above cubicle number four was still out. It really should have been fixed by now, she thought to herself... She stubbed out her cigarette, finished her coffee, picked up another token, and served herself a second coffee. She sat back down, lit another cigarette, and looked at her watch. She still had fifteen minutes before she had to begin work.

She took a long swig of her coffee before swivelling her head round to look at the clock on the wall behind her. It was still broken. Possibly it wasn't completely broken, maybe it just required a new battery. But, she reflected, 33:01 was no good to anybody. And so, whatever the matter with it might be, Sandra made a mental note to report that to the electrician as well.

When a new client was admitted, a senior member of staff would give him a talk and a tour. Then the new client would be left in Sandra's care at the Relaxation Zone, prior to being led to the Medication Room.

She had learnt quite early on that her job was, well, quite simply that, namely just to do her job and no more. She was not there to ask questions or understand the whys and the wherefores of everything. She just had to do her checks and read her data, and basically be there and report anything that she deemed was worthy of reporting – according to the guidelines she had been given.

On the stroke of the hour the data and read-outs would switch over from the night monitor's office to hers. This happened automatically so long as she was in the building, and that was known by her checking in at the main entrance. On the rare occasions that she had not gone into work, once due to a dental appointment and once due to food poisoning, the data would continue to be fed through to the night monitor's office; and when the night monitor finished his shift, instead of the office being locked up for the rest of the day, he would simply be replaced.

Sandra got up and went along the corridor to the toilets. She placed her mug on the washbasin and went over to the end booth. She pulled down her trousers and her knickers and had a pee. After finishing, she washed her hands and gave her mug a rinse under the tap… As she made her way back along the corridor she noticed that another of the strip lights was out in the Long Room. On reaching her office she put her mug into the top drawer of her desk, and looked in the directory for the phone number of the electricians.

"Good morning, this is Sandra from Sector Nine."

"Morning Sandra, what can I do for you then?"

"Two strip lights have gone in the Long Room."

"OK…" began the voice on the other end of the line.

"Three now," interrupted Sandra. There was a display on the wall to the right of Sandra's desk with a plan of all the electrical wiring in her sector. If something mal-functioned, a tiny orange bulb would flash, indicating the operation that needed to be reported.

"That's weird… OK," said the head electrician." I'll send somebody down right away."

"OK, thanks."

Sandra pulled out her chair and sat down. The light on her monitor came on, indicating that the night monitor had just finished his shift and Sandra was just about to begin hers. As she was about to check the read-outs Jasbir came round the corner. Sandra smiled at him through her office panes and then went out to greet him.

"Good morning Jasbir, how are you today?" asked Sandra with a coquettish flutter of the eyelids.

"Pretty good thanks, and yourself?"

"Oh, you know… Anyway, that was pretty quick, by the way."

"What was?"

"Your arrival."

"Oh…" Jasbir smiled, "yeah, I was only up the corridor… in Mr Baum's office. Anyhows, what seems to be the trouble?"

Sandra took him into her office to show him the three flashing orange bulbs. He had a close look at the panel until he was sure he knew the exact location of each of the three lights.

On his way out of her office, Sandra lightly put her hand on Jasbir's shoulder and turned him around so he was facing in the other direction. "And the clock's not working," she said. He looked up at the wall, nodded, and said that he would come back and fix it after he'd repaired the lights.

Sandra watched the gust of vapour escape as Jasbir unlocked and opened the door to the Long Room.

"Right then," Sandra said to herself, as she was finally about to check the morning's readings. But just then the phone rang. "Hello, Sector Nine," said Sandra.

"Good morning Sandra, Ludovik Rubik-Creutzberg here."

"Good morning Mr Rubik-Creutzberg."

"I just wanted to run a couple of things by you."

"Fine."

"Now then, I'm informed that Amy-Lou is off sick."

"Yes, that's right."

"And you're covering her duties till she returns."

"Yes."

"Right… OK. Now I know none of this… er, secretarial, shall we say, stuff is your domain. So, I apologise that we haven't found cover, but…"

"Oh no, that's fine Mr Rubik-Creutzberg. I have all of her relevant files here… She phoned me last week with instr…"

"Very good," interrupted Mr Rubik-Creutzberg. "Umm, right then," he continued, "hold on a minute let me just check… Yeah, number twenty-seven."

"Millman," interjected Sandra.

"Er… yes, that's right… Number twenty-seven, Mr Millman, has twenty-one more days to run before funding runs out, and as of yet we've had no notification… Umm, could you check if there's going to be a re-instigation of funds, or whether we should terminate?"

"I'll do it right away Mr Rubik-Creutzberg."

"Should I maybe give you the relevant contacts?"

"No, that's fine. I've got all the details on the registration documents in Amy-Lou's files."

"Jolly good. And if you could get back to me as soon as you have word…"

"Yes, of course."

"And the other thing", continued Mr Rubik-Creutzberg "is, I'm sure you're aware, number eighteen is due to be pulled today."

"Yes, I know. I thought I'd give it till mid-day, just a little longer, you know… just in case there's a last minute renewal of funding."

"Well…", Mr Rubik-Creutzberg paused for a moment's thought. "Well, of course I leave all this down to your discretion, but I have to say it's not the way I'd go about things. If it were me it would be 9 o'clock on the dot, and bye bye…"

"Yes, but…"

"Don't get me wrong Sandra," interrupted Mr Rubik-Creutzberg. "As I said, you're doing a great job, what with the extra work and everything… you know. And hopefully she'll be back before the end of the week. So, of course, I'll leave all the finer points down to your… but, well, as I say I'm probably harder than you. No no, you carry on, and, er, you know… well done."

"Er, thank you," said Sandra, not really knowing what he was praising her for.

"And, yes, if you could get back to me about number twenty-seven."

"Yes, of course."

"OK, bye for now then."

"Goodbye Mr Rubik-Creutzberg."

Deep inside the icy interior of the Long Room, Jasbir was descending his ladder having changed the bulb in the second light. He put the ladder under his arm and made his way over to the strip light that, according to the readings he now had, he guessed must have a faulty connection somewhere. It seemed as though this particular light, which was above cubicle number four, must have been intermittently flickering on and off for most of the weekend – before finally giving up the ghost.

Meanwhile Sandra searched through her files for the Millman information. She found the forms, copied the contact details down onto a scrap of paper, and returned the file to the cabinet. She was just about to phone the switchboard to request an outside line when Jasbir returned. She put the receiver back down and hid the scrap of paper in the bottom drawer of her desk...

"So?" enquired Sandra, as she closed her office door behind her.

"Nothing to worry about, only bulbs."

"No wiring or anything?"

"No no, just the bulbs."

"That's good."

"Yep."

"If you could just have a look at the clock that'd be fab'."

"No worries, but I think I'll have a coffee first to warm me up."

"I'll join you," said Sandra. "Or..." she continued after a moment's reflection, "maybe I'll have tea this time."

Sandra went into her office to get her mug and a spare one for Jasbir. The coffee machine did supply plastic cups, but who wanted to drink coffee from a plastic cup? She filled the two mugs, put them on the coffee table, and sat down next to Jasbir.

"Good weekend?" asked Jasbir.

"Quiet," replied Sandra.

"Uh huh. You didn't go anywhere with your boyfriend then?"

Sandra gave him a coy little sideways smile and asked: "And how was your weekend?"

"It was my sister's birthday on Saturday, so there was a whole family thing round at my parents'."

"Nice?"

"I guess it was OK… she was thirty."

"Older sister?" enquired Sandra.

"Uh-huh, she's the oldest, then it's me two years younger… I'm in the middle."

"And the youngest?"

"The youngest is Rosheen and she's," Jasbir thought for a moment, "she's twenty six, I think."

"You think?" queried Sandra

"Yeah, no, I mean yes she is twenty-six… What about you?"

"What about me?"

"Sisters, brothers?"

"Oh no, just me."

"Oh, right…" Jasbir thought for a few seconds before saying: "Great lipstick by the way. New?"

"Yes, I got it last Thursday."

"It suits you…" Then after pausing for a moment whilst staring rather too longingly at Sandra's mouth, he continued, "I don't think I've ever seen that shade as a lipstick before."

"Well, thank you. I thought I'd try something completely different… you know, change of image or something."

"Yeah," said Jasbir, and nodded thoughtfully.

"I went a bit mad actually. Thursday after work I bought myself a whole new set of make up; different shades… I just changed everything. Then this weekend I bought new clothes, shoes, everything," continued Sandra enthusiastically, oblivious, as she was, to Jasbir's continued gazing at her – what he considered to be – French pouting Bridget Bardot mouth.

"Bored?" he enquired.

"Um, a bit bored with my wardrobe and everything…"

"No, I meant *bored* 'cos you didn't have anything to do at the weekend… so you decided to go shopping."

"Oh, no no, I'd wanted a quiet weekend," said Sandra. "I was simply, well, I don't know, fed up with the way I looked. Or, not the way I looked exactly, I just felt a bit frumpy… you know. And I hadn't been clothes shopping for ages."

"Right," said Jasbir.

"I found this sort of punky, er, punky-Indiany shop that I'd never seen before. With a mixture of, sort of… seventies stuff and Asian stuff, and batik, and everything."

"Sounds great."

"Uh-huh… and all this weird make up and stuff." She paused before adding, "The shop was called Clockwork Banana. Do you know it?"

Jasbir shook his head.

Sandra gave a little chuckle as if to punctuate the proceedings, stood up, and said, "Excuse me for a moment."

As she made her way over to her office Jasbir decided to have a look at the clock. Sandra's phone began ringing as her hand made contact with her door handle... It was the main gate telling her that she would be getting a stationery delivery at eleven. She looked through the glass in her office door and saw Jasbir up his ladder unhitching the clock from the wall.

She turned to face her screen and placed her hand on its black surface. After several seconds the word 'Authorised' appeared. She punched in her code number and waited. Jasbir was sitting back on the middle sofa with the clock face-down on the seat next to him. Sandra watched him tinkering while she waited for the read-outs to come up on the screen. He had something in his hand, a screwdriver Sandra guessed, with which he was poking the internal workings of the clock.

She turned back to her screen as all the information concerning each of the cubicles was beginning to appear. She waited until the screen was full and began to read. Cubicle 1 – she scanned her eyes quickly along the line of figures – everything normal. Cubicle 2 – yes, yes, yes, everything normal. Cubicle 3 – yes, yes... the temperature gauge was half a degree too high. It was nothing to worry about, it was well within the realms of safety – but it needed to be reported nevertheless.

Sandra picked up the phone and dialled for the technicians. Tridan, who was the only specialist technician she knew by name, said he would be along immediately. She looked at the screen again, more closely this time. She noticed that Cubicle 3 had been wavering between ·5 and 1·2 degrees over the 'flat point' for quite some time...

Friday afternoon, up until she had finished for the weekend, had been a rush. Normally, she would have been notified at least three weeks prior to the admittance of a new client – but on this occasion for some reason she'd been left out of the loop. Either intentionally, or they'd just forgotten to notify her – but she found that difficult to believe. The other possibility, she had mused, was that the new client was a late admittance...

But whatever the reasons for her being notified at such short notice, she had had to get a move on because the new client was going to arrive mid-afternoon... Fortunately for Sandra, Cubicle 4 had already been screened and readied after the previous client had been withdrawn, a few days earlier... Her job was to check that all the readings were being relayed correctly and, since Amy-Lou was on sick leave, set up a separate file for Cubicle 4. She had initially intended to leave all this until the Monday morning, but then after lunch on Friday had decided to get it over with before going home for the weekend. And luckily for her she had; for by the time she was told that the new client was going to arrive later that same day, there would not have been enough time to ready everything prior to his arrival.

With all of this rushing around on the Friday afternoon, she hadn't got around to arranging for the light to be fixed in the Long Room. And by the time everything had been sorted out for the new client, the strip light had completely gone out of her mind. When she did eventually remember, she was on the train home.

Sandra looked over at Jasbir fiddling around with the clock. He looked up and gave her a smile, and Sandra smiled back. He was a sweet person, thought Sandra. A little rough round the edges possibly, but basically a good person. She thought that possibly it was a little sad that the most eventful thing that had occurred in her life recently was that she had been on a large shopping trip. And she wondered whether it would be a good idea to ask Jasbir round to hers for a meal.

Tridan arrived. He did not seem in too much of a hurry. Sandra knew that ·7 of a degree or so over the 'flat point' left plenty of leeway, and wasn't really a big deal. Nonetheless, surely the weekend staff should have noticed it and done something about it.

Tridan spent a couple of minutes greeting Jasbir before going over to Sandra's office.

"Good day to you Sandra," said Tridan as he gave her a rather theatrical salute with his left hand.

"Good morning Tridan," Sandra replied with a smile.

"So, let's have a look at these readings then," he said as he brushed passed her heading for the screen. "Now let's see… Cubicle 3 you said?"

"Yes… but didn't you check the readings at your end?"

"No, there's something weird going on."

"What d'you mean?"

"I dunno really…" Tridan thought for a moment. "Don't say anything, right?" Sandra shook her head. "But I think it's all since those new replacements arrived."

"But…"

"My monitor doesn't work, and there are strange fuzzy half images that occasionally flash up, which are almost too quick for your eye to register."

"You're being para…"

"What? Paranoid?" Tridan interrupted.

"Well, I mean."

"Have you noticed how they all have the same coats?"

"What *are* you talking about?"

"Or, if not identical, very similar."

"Who?"

"The new replacements." Tridan looked out through the glass of Sandra's office. He peered across to the Long Room, then furtively up and down the corridor – and he looked like a Stasi agent waiting to exchange a package for a microfiche. "Now," he continued, "you keep this to yourself, right?" Sandra nodded. "Have you tried phoning any of our former colleagues at home?"

"Well, of course not... I didn't know any of them that well."

"No... well, if you did you'd find out that their phone numbers don't exist."

"Wha..."

"Really. I've tried three of their numbers. Nothing, zilch, nada. I'm telling you – if I were you I'd think about leaving here as quick as you can and never coming back."

"This is madness."

"I'm telling you, there's weird shit going down – I can feel it. And I ain't gonna end up being the deep-fried rat in a southern fried chicken supper."

"So, how come you're still here then?"

Once again, Tridan inspected the scene through Sandra's windows – and looked like a novice who was about to rob a bank. "This is my last day," he said, with his index finger held up to his lips. "From this evening I'll be un-contactable..."

"Well..." began Sandra.

"Look, you just think about it, yeah? I'm telling you... you know... just feel the vibes yourself, and you'll know I'm right."

Sandra didn't say anything, but was pretty sure that Tridan was nuts. She recalled how on one occasion Tridan had gone on for ages about the Americans having never sent a man to the moon. And another time, only a couple of weeks after she'd been working there, he was saying something about how a month before JFK's death Jackie Onassis had visited Salvador Dalí in Spain. And although Tridan hadn't found a connection yet he was convinced that Jackie's clandestine visit and Kennedy's death were linked in some way…

Yes, Sandra was sure that he was one of those people who saw a conspiracy around every corner. But nonetheless, just to eliminate any element of doubt, she vowed to get hold of some of the ex-employees' home telephone numbers, and give a few of them a ring that evening. Just to be sure…

"Are the Cubicles OK?" Sandra must have sounded anxious, because Tridan turned from the screen to look up at her and give her a reassuring smile.

"Don't worry honey," he said as he turned his attention back to the read outs "…up to, um, one… one-and-a-half degrees, is fine." But just as the last syllable of his sentence had left his mouth he screamed out "Shiiiiiiiiiiiiiiiiiiiiitttt!"

"What? What's the matter?" Sandra cried back.

"Number 4, Cubicle number 4. Look! Look! Brain activity… there's been brain activity. There shouldn't be *any* brain activity at all!"

Sandra scrambled to peer over his shoulder. She stared at the readings in disbelief. First her mouth dropped limply open, then, with a louder sound than had ever been emitted from her mouth before, she hollered: "Nooooooooooooooooooooooooo!"

XVII

(Part II)

I took the remnants of my coffee and stood in the passageway. I watched as the outskirts of London transformed into the roads, buildings, flyovers, and people of the capital. The announcer announced that we would shortly be arriving at our destination. I had not been to London for a long time; I had had no reason to until now…

    Unsure, as if in a dream, I watched as the trees turned into lampposts and the buildings got taller… We juddered to a halt and I let the other passengers alight first before bumping my rucksack down the steps and onto the platform. I carried my rucksack in front of me and made my way over to a vacant bench. I rested it against the seat and sat down. Was I being crazy, I wondered? Maybe I should get on the next train to the airport and just get out of there – out of this mad city with its mad ideas.

    Unfortunately, I was not crazy. I had thought it all through long and hard, and I did not really have a choice. And maybe I would wake up and be in a dream; maybe I would be in a nightmare. I hoped it would be a dream though… I threw my head back and exhaled a sudden deep breath that made my cheeks puff out, which in turn left me with an open mouthed smile on my face. How ridiculous this all was, but the time for thinking was over.

I turned my head to the side and leaned over the edge of the bench I was sitting on. I coughed five, six, seven times and spat. The spit was green with red flecks in it – and I knew I didn't really have a choice…

As I heaved my rucksack up and onto the seat, and turned and bent forward to stick my arms through the straps, a vision of loveliness passed by: tight flower print slacks, over-sized un-tucked white shirt, a fraying blue denim jacket, and a smile seemingly for no reason at all… On another day at another time? Possibly… It was a good thought. But, it was not another day, and it was not another time.

I walked on and watched her bottom ripple as she advanced down the platform. I reached into my pocket for my train ticket. A fountain of silver cascaded to the ground as coins of varying denominations fell to the floor: a hurried rush of circular escapees bidding for freedom. The dulled sound of metallic rainfall that the coins made on hitting the platform, and hitting each other, provoked the woman in the flower print trousers to turn around. As I bent forward our eyes met. She smiled with lips that encased a voice I was certain was incapable of lies; and then she parted, possibly sensing that today was not the day…

One of the coins had rolled its coiled path over the edge of the platform and under the frozen train. As I heaved myself back to the vertical, I wondered how long it would lie there amongst the stones and debris. Possibly it would be there for many years. At first losing its value and then ending up being worth hundreds of times what the mint had initially envisaged.

I happily willed distractions on my mind, for what else was I to do? It was early, but that was the way it had to be… I made my way towards the ticket barrier and watched as the woman in the denim jacket handed over her proof of purchase to a woman in a peaked cap. She looked familiar, but there had been no hint of recognition as our eyes had met. Maybe she reminded me of someone, or possibly it was her clothes. Or maybe she just looked like somebody I would like to meet. I handed over my ticket to the woman in the unnecessary uniform and considered the next steps of my journey: Underground, train, bus…

There seemed to be more people than I remembered, but maybe that was the time of day, or the time of year; or the way my mind was readying itself. I was hungry and thirsty, and I was nervous – but that was the way it had to be... And my mind was having uncharacteristic thoughts.

I stepped down from the bus into what was becoming a beautiful sunny Friday afternoon. Countryside was near and the smell of freshly mown grass hung delicately in the warm summer air. I posted my fourteen letters in the post-box that was guarding the bus shelter. The red Double Decker pulled away and I was left on my own heading towards trees and hillocks. I felt sick, an aching hollow sickness that forced acid up into the back of my throat. I burped as a burning sensation in my chest made me wince. This was all normal, I told myself.

A few metres ahead, off to my left, I spied a village pond surrounded by ducks waiting for a purpose, and I tried to force myself to think about birds and then amphibians for a moment. And as I passed alongside, I noticed a small hut on an island in the middle of the pond with a sign attached to it that read Duckingham Palace... But I did not smile. Because smiling, like gambling, is for fools or people in situations other than mine. And it would have made no odds whether I had a marked deck in my pocket or a solitary ace of spades. Either way, I knew that the day had come when I had to look into the devil's eyes and call his bluff... Just so long as I could hold my nerve.

The road gradually narrowed and the pavements became grass verges. I let a wooden pylon take some of the weight from my back as I checked the directions I'd been sent through the post. It was a perfect summer's day, still and fresh, peaceful and quiet. On days like these, it was hard to imagine that anything was wrong with the world. I looked over to the rolling hills in the distance, with their clumps of trees and acrylic green grass; and to the other side, with its meadows and fields of varying hues haphazardly defined by a tangled array of bushes and bramble that respected otherwise all-but-forgotten ancient territorial claims.

This was picture postcard Britain. A Britain of cream teas and triangular sandwiches, cricket on the village green and freckled twenty-somethings in soft flowing summer dresses who refrain from sex before marriage… This was not the real Britain though. Of course, these little enclaves of conservativism with a small 'C' and Empire with a big 'e' did still exist, but these people were no more than pitiful solipsist figures of ridicule. Woeful creatures removed from any sense of the here and now, living in a time warp based on an idea of an era that never existed. These are the sad ones that cannot quite follow everything you are saying to them, so antiquated are their thought processes and so removed are their points of reference.

There are the vicious ones as well though, the bovver boys of the flower arranging set: the ones who are not decent enough to remain in their Jurassic strongholds; the ones that see it fit to forthrightly push their nostalgia for nothing – unfortunately too lacking in intelligence to realise how ignorant they are. But *these* were the minorities that would eventually get wiped out.

And as I stood there feeling kind of seasick, looking over an ocean of yellows and greens, I knew that the best thing about Britain was that it was eclectic. It was brown and black and Celtic and English and yellow and white; and the very fact that Britishness was difficult to define was what made it *great*. That is what Britain was, late trains and Monty Python. Not fitting into boxes, not having rigid hard definitions for what belonged where. Things just were. They had evolved so, and the unpredictability of it all – the weather included – was what this land was all about.

I wanted a coffee and my legs felt wobbly. I rolled a cigarette – nobody had said anything about cigarettes. My directions told me that I was very close now. And on a day like today, in this land of stone circles and Norman castles, I wished I could do a little more exploring and reacquainting. Another time, a different time, when I had more time… I took a left through a carts-width break in a densely forested section of the roadside. There was no sign. The wood was long and dense and once I was the other side, a pathway led me through a large field. The pathway eventually took me to a large gate, which was the entrance to a compound, which was surrounded by intimidating looking fencing.

I turned my head to look back at the wood and the field I had just traversed, but I knew there was no turning back.

"Hello there," said the entrance guard as I approached.

"Hello, I've come to see Mr Rubik-Creutzberg or Ms Pitts," I told him as I handed over my documentation.

"Yes, you're expected." He handed the documents back to me and beckoned me through the slowly opening gate. He came out of his kiosk and held out his hand, which I shook. He then escorted me to a covered parking lot, which looked like a large cow shed; its doors were great black hanging flaps of rubber, like an abattoir's. It was stuffy inside, airless and unwelcoming. The guard led me up to one of the fifteen or so futuristic looking metallic golf type buggies, which I was told were known as 'Spuggies' – short for space buggy. They were futuristic in the way those 1950s sci-fi magazines had viewed the future: awkward, colourful, and optimistic, with rounded-off edges.

The guard helped me off with my rucksack, which he plonked in the back of the first Spuggy we came to. I sat inside, he punched in a few numbers on the dashboard, said goodbye, and I was off. The rubber doors automatically parted and I was once again out in the warm summer sunlight. The buggy zipped along at a good pace – to the right first, and then along the side of the compound. About a third of the way along, the buggy took a left and slowly approached a ramp that led up to two thick metal doors. Once inside the building the Spuggy progressed at a more sedate pace, along the brightly lit antiseptic looking corridor. And after three or four minutes it pulled to a standstill in front of an office door.

The whole journey must have taken a little under ten minutes. The buggy's left door opened and I got out. I heaved my rucksack over the back edge of the buggy and leaned it against the wall. The corridor was empty save for the office door. I looked around and felt like crying; but this was not a time for sadness. This was a time for rejoicing – after all, I had been fortunate to be taken on at all. If it hadn't been for my uncle having worked here for all those years, there was no way I'd have heard about the place – let alone been accepted… And anyway, what could I have done in two or three months? Not a great deal. No, this really was my only option.

Just then, the office door opened. A completely bald gentleman in a jazzy pin-striped suit, who was approximately fifty-five, appeared.

"Good morning, I'm Mr Rubik-Creutzberg, please do come in," he said with a warm smile as he shook my hand.

The next hour and a half consisted of an introductory talk, plenty of form filling in, an in-depth psychological question and answer session, conducted by a rather sexy long-legged Icelandic woman with fluffy white hair, and brief scientific and legal explanations of what I was about to embark upon. I paid up for twenty-three years and stated on the accompanying form where any additional funding – if additional funding was needed – could be obtained. Mr Rubik-Creutzberg carefully read what I had written, and asked several questions concerning my text. Some of my replies prompted him to add the occasional sentence or two in the margin, which he asked me to read and initial if I was in complete agreement with his clarifications.

He smiled as he deliberately raised himself by pushing down on the two arms of his chair. I was led along corridor upon corridor. First left, then right, then left again... Some were wide corridors like the one in which Mr Rubik-Creutzberg's office was located; and some were narrow, only just wide enough for us to walk abreast. All of them were sanatorium white and brightly lit... For the duration, Mr Rubik-Creutzberg made small talk. I was fully aware of what he was trying to do, but I was happy for it nevertheless. I wondered how I looked to him. If I looked terrified it did not register on his face. And I considered how many times Mr Rubik-Creutzberg had walked these corridors with a newly paid up intern, and how he could take it all so matter-of-factly... I guess he was confident in what he was doing.

"First of all let me say that I knew your Uncle very well... Yes yes, it was a great loss. Very sorry, um... we were *all* very sorry. Quite unexpected as well..." Mr Rubik-Creutzberg paused for a moment. Then his eyes widened slightly as his unkempt eyebrows rose. And then, as we progressed at an unhurried pace along the white corridors, his head quickly turned to me and he said, "Would you like to see him?" But I simply shook my head and grimaced at the thought – immediately dispelling any sense of enthusiasm he may have had for his bizarre proposition. "No no, of course not, silly of me... One day, umm?" he said with what I guessed was his approximation of a reassuring smile. "Now then, I saw from your application form that you've done a lot of travelling. That's marvellous, wonderful really. I haven't done as much as I would have liked. Oh, you know, I meant to, of course I meant to. But, well, then Mrs Rubik-Creutzberg came along, and then the kids, and you know how it is. Of course, we go for a two-week holiday once a year – France usually. But, I mean, it just doesn't compare to what you've been doing. No no, very envious. It all sounds fascinating; very good for the spirit I'm sure. Yes yes, very fortunate indeed... Dear me, here I am fifty-seven and hardly been outside the UK. Not good that, not good at all... quite embarrassing really... but, well, you know what they say, never too late. Who knows maybe one day... Actually, I've always wanted to visit..." And that was how Mr Rubik-Creutzberg carried on for the entire walk.

As we turned a corner I saw a woman hurriedly come out of a door to the right, cross the corridor and disappear from view to the left. I was soon able to see that the room from which the woman had darted was long, cold looking, and full of telephone sized kiosks... As we advanced I could see an office to my left, where the woman now sat at a desk; and a little after that was a wider space where three sofas were at right angles to each other around a coffee table – and my mind was racing.

Mr Rubik-Creutzberg instructed me to sit down for several moments in the Relaxation Zone. The sight of an ashtray made me roll up a cigarette.

"Is Number 4 ready?" Mr Rubik-Creutzberg asked the woman who had come out of her office to greet him.

"Yes, all ready to go Mr Rubik-Creutzberg," she replied.

"I won't be a moment," he said to me as he walked along the corridor. I nodded and lit my cigarette with trembling hands.

"Hi there I'm Sandra," said the attractive woman with the strange coloured lipstick.

"Hello," I replied.

"Don't worry, everybody's nervous, but there's never a hitch... Where are you from Mr..." Just then, Mr Rubik-Creutzberg returned and signalled for me to follow him. As I got up I glanced above the drinks machine that was against the wall, to look at the clock. I wanted to know at what precise time my future was going to begin. But the damn thing clearly had a wiring problem because all it was flashing up was one minute past thirty-three. Oh well, I thought, three o'clock was as good a guess as any. Three o'clock, Friday July 3rd ... this was the date and time I would try to keep in my mind.

"Bye bye then," said Sandra as she put her arm around my shoulder and squeezed it reassuringly.

"Er, bye Sandra," I mumbled with tears in my eyes, as I hastily stubbed out my cigarette in the half full ashtray.

I followed Mr Rubik-Creutzberg along the corridor to a door marked Medication Room. Mr Rubik-Creutzberg shook my hand and said, "Well, if I don't see you again all the best for the future."

"Er, yes... thank you," and I burst into tears.

Mr Rubik-Creutzberg patted me on the back a couple of times and held the Medication Room's door open for me. I walked through in a daze, feeling as though a Jimi Hendrix song was planted in my brain, and that all this was happening to somebody else. My mind was unable to get a grip on anything tangible. None of this had any meaning for me. It was all foreign, beyond my realms of comprehension. I was in an alien land about to do something to myself that my primal instincts were searching to comprehend.

Maybe I needed more time to think, to reconsider, and to weigh up the alternatives. But there was no more time and there were no alternatives. I was too ill, too sick. And any misguided hope that a cure would be found within the next few months, was just that: misguided. Like looking for gold in a disused Cornish tin mine, it was all but hopeless... And while I still looked alright, and its grip hadn't completely taken hold, and there would still be a me worth reviving, I had to do this thing *now* – before it really was too late.

"If you wouldn't mind just lying here," said the man in the white coat. I did as I was asked; for my mind was no longer capable of doing anything other than follow instructions. And I felt shivery, uncontrollably so.

I lay down, accompanied by my strange thoughts and my sense of isolation. And my capacity for reason would have flown out of the window, had there been one. But in this old-style futuristic minimalist compound, which reminded me of a building from the Soviet Bloc, no light was allowed in – and no thoughts could fly away to the freedom of the double-decker highway.

The man dressed all in white attached a plastic wristband around my left wrist with a number four on it. "Don't worry sir," he said, as he peered down on me from what appeared to be far away, but couldn't have been. And as he turned to face the other way checking instruments on a silver tray, he said: "Science is advancing all the time… some say that the know-how is already here, it's just being kept secret for the moment."

The music gently piped its way through the speakers set into the walls. It was a gentle wallpaper sound that was meant to relax you, no doubt, and take the edge off what was really happening. I moved my head slightly to one side, stared at the black egg-shaped clock on the work surface to my right, and allowed my introspections and regrets to take hold.

I thought about the women I'd loved and lost, and about the women I'd loved and not wanted to lose. I recalled my train journey to this place, and the gnawing loneliness from time running out that I'd felt… Images of my time in Leipzig passed through my mind like a flickering zoetrope: the Trabant I'd bought myself; the old watchmaker who'd lived next door to me and had died before being able to return my watch, and the bust of Lenin I'd found in a skip in front of our apartment block a couple of days after his funeral – no doubt discarded by a younger generation of his relatives who had no time for nostalgia or history… And I recalled all of those interminable visits to soviet style constructivist hospitals in the former East Germany, where, I suppose, I finally made the decision that determined my fate.

Most of all, as my bones felt as though they were melting, I thought about the end of ideology, the end of self, and the end of time…

The man turned around and approached with what looked to me to be the largest needle I had ever seen. I began to shake more violently. And like a rock 'n' roll star regretting having tried for some kind of asphyxiated high, my mind screamed out "No!" as the needle penetrated my left upper arm.

XVIII

I sat at my desk with my pad in front of me. I looked out of my window and watched as the white cube undulated and spun away. Getting smaller and smaller as it danced and swayed over the roofs and chimneys of the nighttime city, until it looked as if it was the size of a die in the distance – and then it was gone... I strained my eyes for a few seconds, but I somehow knew I had seen the last of it.

I turned my focus back to my pad, with its thousands and thousands of words, and pressed my pen down hard at the end of the last line. I gently placed my pen next to the paper. I crossed my arms on my desk, lay my head on top, closed my eyes, and smiled... I had written the final full stop.

THE END

GLOSSARY

ERLÄUTERUNGEN

1. **Intershop** - Intershops were shops in the former East Germany that only sold Western goods. Since only Western currencies were accepted in these shops, they were predominantly frequented by tourists or travelling business people. Those from East Germany (the DDR) who were fortunate enough to have some West German money (it often being sent through the post by family members who lived in the West) would also be able to purchase goods in the Intershops.

There were between eight and ten Intershops in Leipzig in East German times: One in each of the large hotels in Leipzig (of which there were five), one in the Central Station, one in the city centre, and one at the International Exhibition Centre (the *Messe*), for example…

2. **Moccamix** - Moccamix or Mixcafe cost 8.75 Ost Marks (the East German currency) for a 125 gram packet. It was a mix of real coffee and roasted barley.

3. **Zenit** - A Zenit camera was a good quality camera manufactured in the Soviet Union.

4. **Sozialismus deine Welt** - Sozialismus deine Welt (Socialism Your World), was the name of the book presented to each child in the DDR on turning fourteen years old... At some stage during the child's fourteenth year a mass celebration for all who had recently turned fourteen years old would be organised by their school (where the book Sozialismus deine Welt would be presented). After which each child would go home to have another, this time, private celebration amongst family and friends.

Becoming fourteen was a big thing during East German times, and is still celebrated in the eastern part of Germany to this day. It was a non-religious rites of passage called a Jugendweihe, when a child became an adult. To the extent that after a 'child's' Jugendweihe, teachers in school would ask the individual which form of the 'You' pronoun they would subsequently wish to be addressed (the German language has two words for 'You': Du and Ihr. The former is informal used to address friends and children, for example; the latter is formal, and used when talking to people you do not know, or wish to show respect towards. Or, in the case of a child, it is the form employed when conversing with an adult.

5. **Sprachlos** - Was a brand of East German cigarettes. It is translated as Speechless.

6. **Spartakiade** - Can most easily be described as an Eastern Bloc version of the Olympics.

7. **Hell** - An East German beer.

8. **Ost Mark** - The East German currency was divided into Marks (Ost Marks) and Pfennige. One Ost Mark was the equivalent of one hundred Pfennige (Pf)...

In DDR Times:

The Average Monthly Wage	-	800 to 900 Marks
Price of a Trabant Car	-	13,000 Marks
Price of a Colour TV	-	6,000 Marks
Price of a Mono Tape Recorder and Radio	-	1,160 Marks
Price of a Tape Recorder without Radio	-	500 Marks
Monthly rent for an all inclusive Flat for 2 or 3 people	-	45 Marks
Beer, 0.25 l, in a bar (mainly 'Hell' or Pilsner beer)	-	40 Pf
Lemonade	-	20 Pf
Bockwurst sausage with bread	-	85 Pf
Grillette (a toasted sausage and cheese sandwich)	-	1 Mark
A return trip to Cuba (going by plane and returning by cruise ship)	-	10,000 Marks
1 kg of Mushrooms	-	16 Marks
Tram tickets for a journey of any distance: Adult	-	20 Pf
Child	-	10 Pf
For an evening out in a pub with enough food to fill you up and enough alcohol to get you drunk	-	10 Marks

N.B. From the mid 1970s till the end of the DDR prices did not change.

9. Leaders of the German Democratic Republic

(i) Willhelm Pieck   1949-1960

(ii) Walter Ulbricht	1960-1973
(iii) Willi Stoph	1973-1976
(iv) Erich Honecker	1976-1989
(v) Egon Krenz	October 1989-November 1989
------------------------------------	------------------------------
(vi) Manfred Gerlach and Hans Modrow	1989-1990
(vii) Sabine Bergmann and, Lothar de Maiziere	1990-3rd October 1990 1990-End

Wilhelm Pieck – is seen as having been a very friendly man. An anti-fascist. In people's minds, the post-war end of rationing is inextricably linked with his premiership. The war years had been long and hard, and he was a symbol of hope and optimism for a brighter future. He instigated and oversaw vast new house building programmes.

Walter Ulbricht – was a hardliner. A Stalinist. It was during his time that television aerials facing the West were broken down. During his leadership long hair for men was not really permitted, and jeans in some schools were forbidden (although this depended on the school and the Head); both of these policies were difficult to enforce.

In discos, in the latter days of the DDR, one track from the West could be played for every three from the Eastern Bloc (not that this was particularly adhered to)... Whereas, during Ulbricht's reign no Western music was allowed whatsoever.

His famous statement on the subject was "we don't need this yeah yeah yeah music". During the 1960s in Leipzig, there was a demonstration against the banning of 'Beat' music. The police came and made the demonstrators take off and give them their jeans – in exchange for which the demonstrators were given horrible pairs of trousers to go home in.

Willi Stoph – was there for such a short time that he did not really influence anything. He did little more than keep things ticking over.

If anything can be said about him, it is that he was certainly more liberal than Ulbricht had been.

Erich Honecker – was considerably better than Walter Ulbricht had been. Beat music was more accepted. He opened things up to quite an extent. Several internationally renowned bands played in East Germany, for example.

The thing with Honecker was that he appeared to have this continual societal pincer movement going on. That is to say, he would open things up, then, for whatever reason, when he believed that society was going too far in that direction, he would close things up again. This was constantly the way with Honecker – free things up then pull in the reins slightly.

Towards the end of his premiership he was simply too old and lacked new ideas.

Egon Krenz – was in power far too short a time to assess either what his views were or what kind of a leader he might have become.

When considering the DDR, one would not be fundamentally incorrect if one simply cited the above five men as having been the only leaders of the German Democratic Republic. However, history in reality seldom has neat encyclopaedic definitions or clearly drawn beginnings and ends. Thus, although it would be a much more easily considered concept had the last day of the DDR been when the Berlin Wall came down – this was not the case. Hence, we have (vi) and (vii).

These first five Presidents of the DDR were pretty much the embodiment of everything. They were, for example, 'The General Secretary of the Central Committee of the S.E.D' (the S.E.D. was the East German Socialist Party); the 'Head of the Staatsrat of the DDR' (the Staatsrat was the body of top ministers that made up the government); and the 'Head of National Defence'. Between 1946 and 1989, other influential positions did exist, but, almost without exception, the real power resided in the hands of the President.

During this period a combination of the fact that everything was changing so rapidly and nobody really knew what was going to happen, coupled with the fact that overall power no longer remained in one single person's hands (the Socialist party had lost its all embracing influence, for example) – meant that hereafter two people can be seen to have had the power and authority:

Manfred Gerlach (Volkskammer President[10]) and,

Hans Modrow (Political Chief). Then, subsequently,

Sabine Bergmann (Volkskammer Pesident) and,

Lothar de Maiziere (Political Chief).

The Political Chief of East Germany had always come from the Socialist Party ie the S.E.D. (which later became the P.D.S.). Lothar de Maiziere was both the first 'democratically' elected Political Chief of the D.D.R., and he was the first Political Chief to come from outside of the Socialist Party. He came from the C.D.U. (which is the centre right party of Germany).

10. **The Volkskammer President** - The Volkskammer President or The People's room President, was the chief of the DDR's equivalent of parliament.

11. **AKA** - AKA was an East German electrical appliances manufacturer.

12. **Stern** - Stern, meaning Star, was one of the makes of East German Radio Cassette Recorders.

13. **Cars in East German times** - To get a new car in DDR times you would have to go to the IFA Vertrieb Auto Anmeldung office. It was a tiny little office in Leipzig, maybe ten metres squared. Its function was to register you for the fourteen year waiting list for a new car.

You had to be at least eighteen years old to put yourself down on the waiting list; so, often a friendly grandmother, for example, would register in your place when you were a child and switch over the registration forms when you came of age. Or, purchase the car in your place and give it to you when the fourteen years were up.

If, when your particular waiting time had elapsed, there were some of the Western models available (Volvo; VW Golf; or Mazda 323) you could change the order that you had registered yourself for, all those years previously. For example, if you were in line to receive a Lada you could pay a little bit more and have a VW Golf.

14. **Broiler Bar** - Broiler was the East German word for a chicken. A word unknown in the West German language. Hence, a Broiler Bar was where people went extensively to eat chicken, although other food was available, and maybe have a beer or two before going on somewhere else. Broiler Bars no longer exist.

15. **Nikolaikirche** - The Nikolaikirche is the church in the centre of Leipzig, which played such an intrinsic part in the demise of the East German system. The sign outside the church, which is still there to this day, reads "Nikolaikirche offen für alle" which meant that the Nikolai church was open for all. The Church in DDR times should not so much be seen as solely a religious organisation as much as a focus for dissent. Every Monday evening from 1980 there were small meetings in the church that were not uniquely religious, addressing, as they did, problems and complaints about certain issues related to the DDR régime. Towards the end of the East German system the numbers congregating at the Nikolaikirche were too great to all fit inside the church and had to

spill over onto the streets outside. What had begun as small gatherings grew larger and larger from one Monday to the next. It was in August of 1989 that these Monday meetings transformed into the first demonstration around the city centre. Soon other towns and cities in the DDR were to follow with their own demonstrations. On the 7th October 1989, it was the German Democratic Republic's annual National Day of Celebration. Gorbechev went to Berlin as honoured guest. He and Honecker greeted each other by embracing; however, during Gorbechev's speech he cryptically criticised the DDR régime by saying that those who do not change are punished. Whether or not Honecker understood what Gorbechev was getting at is unclear; what is clear is that the 'people' understood full well, and took it as a sign.

On October 9th, the Monday, Leipzig experienced its largest ever demonstration, 300,000 strong walking around the Inner Ring road of the city centre. As they walked they chanted two things: firstly, "Gorbi, Gorbi …" (for Gorbechev) because he had basically refused to send the Soviet tanks in; and secondly, "we are the people …" (because in DDR times everything was done 'in the name of the people'). Several days later Erich Honecker was replaced by Egon Krenz. Jumped or pushed? Probably pushed by the higher echelons of the S.E.D. Then, on 11th November 1989 the Berlin Wall came down.

16. **The Polish Information Bureau** - In DDR times it was difficult to get hold of Western music. As soon as a batch of records came in they went. In addition to which, lots of Western groups were banned. Not in a consistent way however. For example, The Rolling Stones were banned; however once they started speaking out against the Vietnam War they were back in favour for a while. At the Polish Information Bureau, situated in the centre of Leipzig, one could purchase either banned or hard to get hold of records from under the counter.

17. **The wide inner ring by-pass** - This wide three to five laned road which encircled Leipzig's city centre, is the road that the marchers walked around on their demonstrations in the latter days of the DDR.

18. **Nina Hagen** - a well known East German singer/songwriter punk with an operatic voice who defected to the West towards the end of the 1970s.

19. **Unverkäufliches Beratungsmuster** - This was the sign that could occasionally be seen in shop windows. It basically meant that the display in the window was only a display and could not be purchased inside the shop.

20. **Alexander Platz** - Alexander Platz is the large square that was the centre of the former East Berlin.

21. **Genex geld** - In the last years of the East German system instead of citizens being able to purchase goods from Intershops[1] directly, with West German money, as had previously been the case, they had to exchange their Western currency for Genex money first.

22. **Cash point card** - A little known fact is that from the mid-eighties the DDR had several cash point machines. These could only be found in the largest towns and cities though.

23. **The Berlin Wall** - The Berlin Wall, officially known in the DDR as the Antifaschistischer Schutzwall, which means 'Anti-fascist Protection Wall', was begun to be built on the 12th August 1961.

24. **Checkpoint Charlie** - Checkpoint Charlie is the most well known of the East/West border crossings in Berlin. Any DDR citizens who could cross from East to West always had to use other border crossings. Checkpoint Charlie was only for tourists or foreign nationals.

25. **Wer will, dass die Welt so bleibt wie sie ist, der will nicht, dass sie bleibt** - He who wants the world to survive as it is does not want the world to survive at all.

26. **The Russian Sector** - Berlin was split up into four sectors. East Berlin was the Russian Sector; and West Berlin was divided up into the British, American, and French Sectors respectively.

27. **A Grillette** - A Grillette was sausage and cheese in between two slices of toast.

28. **Quietschpappe** - There are certain words that are quintessentially East German. This is just such a word. What it in fact means is Styrofoam, the West German word for which is Styropur. 'Quietsch' is actually a noise such as squelch or squeak, and 'Pappe' is paper. Hence 'Quietschpappe' means squeakpaper.

29. **Die Runde Ecke** - Die Runde Ecke (The Round Corner) was the building in Leipzig that was the headquarters of the Stasi (the East German secret police). Its name came from the fact that it was situated on a sweeping round corner just off the city centre's inner ring road. It can now be visited, with its post room for steaming open letters and ironing them closed shut again; and its exhibition of concealed cameras in the likes of cigarette packets and false stomachs. The most poignant part of the display is when one is leaving. On the wall is a photograph of demonstrators on the steps in front of the building, taken in the last year of the DDR. The demonstrators are holding up a banner or Wink Element[34] which reads: "When will this place become a museum?".

30. **The Stasi** - The Stasi were the East German secret police. 'Stasi' stood for Staatssicherheit.

31. **Im Nu** - Im Nu means 'straight away' or 'suddenly'. It was, and still is, a popular East German malt drink.

32. **The DDR National Football Team** - East Germany only played West Germany once in an international football match. It was in 1974, and East Germany won 1-0.

33. **FDJ** - Was the East German Communist youth organisation. 'FDJ' stood for Freie Deutsche Jugend.

34. **Wink Element** - A Wink Element is a uniquely East German term that means banner. 'Wink' comes from the verb winken which means 'to wave'.

Notes and Acknowledgements

The song lyric quoted on page 24 is from 'Ashes to Ashes' by David Bowie (published by RCA records), as released on *Scary Monsters (and Super Creeps)* (1980).

'Zig Zag Wanderer', referred to on page 50, is a reference to the song of the same name, by Captain Beefheart and his Magic Band, from the album *Safe as Milk* (1967), (published by Buddah Records).

The painting described on page 156 is 'Sunrise by the Ocean' by Vladimir Kush.

The list of the numbers and types of inhabitants in Berlin, which appears on page 102/3, was taken from *Der Spiegel* magazine, circa 1996-97.

During the writing of this novel I was listening to lots of East and West German music, such as: Einstürzende Neubauten; Feeling B; Herbst in Peking; Die Ärzte; Can; Faust; Amon Düül II; NEU!, and, Harmonia...

Although 'A Certain Experience of the Impossible' was my first published novel, it was the manuscript I wrote second. It is this one, 'Lines Within the Circle', that was my first attempt at writing a novel. I probably began writing it in about 2000 or 2001, in Leipzig, in the former East Germany. But it is only about one year ago that I retrieved it from the bottom of a drawer to look at it again...

I wish to thank the following people:

Evelyn Czichos – for making me so happy during this period in Leipzig, and for her editing skills and suggestions concerning this manuscript, and above all for her love; Morfydd Bonnin for all her help, advice, and love, and for being the best mother anyone could hope to have; Janet Hummel – for all the work she put into this first manuscript of mine; Andy Griffiths – for his friendship and technical help; Peter ten Eicken – for being a great friend who enjoyed crazy adventures and Portuguese life as much as I did; André Schultze, Ronald Koetteritzsch, Anke Gerlach, Jörg Zschage, Connie Claus, and Steffen Webber – for their friendship and for checking that the details I included about East Germany were correct; and, Alex Reed – for being the most imaginative, unique, and fun-loving musician I know, and for being a good friend who has always been ready for an absurdist adventure.

And for reasons they will be aware of, my gratitude also goes to:

Johnny Segers; Bob and Indrani Curry; Nick and Sarah Pope; Sam Chally; Nicole Hase; Yvelaine Armstrong; Jodi Brooke; Andrew Startup; 'ö-Dzin Tridral; Ingrid Murphy; and the outer rings of Saturn.

Special thanks go to Kathy, Caroline, Anette, and John.

Jean Bonnin
Pembrokeshire,
December 2011

V5i

Red Egg Publishing – are a new publishing company. We are interested in the quirky, the radical, the imaginative, and the offbeat.

We wish to support the struggling writer, the original thinker, and the wordsmith who is too unconventional (whatever that means) to have a chance of being considered for publication by the mainstream publishing houses…

We want to promote good writing in all its forms – writing that addresses issues in an innovative, intelligent, amusing, and thought-provoking manner.

We welcome submissions.

For novels – please email your contact details, a short biography, and a synopsis, as part of your email (not as separate attachments)… If we enjoy what we read we'll request the first 50 pages or first three chapters.

Please send everything via the website: www.redeggpublishing.com

Thank you,

Red Egg

For more information about Jean Bonnin: www.jeanbonnin.com

Lightning Source UK Ltd.
Milton Keynes UK
UKOW04f0315020315

247124UK00001B/35/P